*Say
Hello*

Say Hello

Katy Stanton

atmosphere press

for my sisters

Meg

Out on the street today, some homeless guy shouts at me, "Do you know that you've been saved?" I can smell his sour breath. My heart starts beating faster, and I run—stumble, really—back to the house. The whole episode freaked me out, but all day, I keep hearing that old guy's question in my head.

I could have told him, *I do know I've been saved.* I was saved exactly one hundred thirty-two days ago. One hundred thirty-two days and counting.

One hundred thirty-two days ago, I was supposed to get married. I was supposed to wear my mother's lacy wedding gown and make my sisters wear royal blue bridesmaid dresses. Dad was supposed to walk me down the aisle. Getting married was supposed to make everything right again. But I didn't get married, I got *saved* instead. My hero snatched me right from the jaws of the angry yellow dragon.

All this might sound crazy. A sordid fairy tale. A lurid soap opera. Too bizarre to be true. But with my heart beating too fast and my whole body still feeling the breath of the angry dragon, I want to tell my story.

Six years before
at home in Maryland
My sister Meg's story and mine
intersect in a country farmhouse.
We grew up as Farrah Fawcett's
picture
in a red swimsuit
made millions.
My sister Meg wanted
her golden hair to look just like Farrah's
and spent hours trying. I can picture her
practicing a big white smile
in the mirror.

Meg was the pretty one--
smart and funny and fearless.
I admired her,
but that doesn't mean we got along.
Just like the Beatles song--
she'd say goodbye,
and I'd say hello.
Like somehow, we were opposite
sides of the same coin.
Sometimes I'd feel her stare
and she'd ask,
"How can you just *sit* there?"
I didn't understand.
I'd ask, "What?"

"How can you just sit there and read? Don't you want to
    go *do* something?"
"I am *doing* something.
Leave me alone," I'd tell her.
She would finally leave.

There was also the third sister.
Our younger sister, Mia, was special.
Special needs, special attention,
just special.
There is no true label for Mia.
She is the only one of her kind.
Did she really run naked across the street?
Oh, yes.
She would bite her own arm
when frustrated until she left
marks and bruises. She could spoil a party or sleepover
with too much crying or too much laughter.
It took a year to teach her to say, Mee-Ahh. Mee-Ahh.
This is supposed to be Meg's story,
but even this story drifts to Mia--the cute little pixie
fireball who takes over everything.

Being the oldest sister,
my role was easy to play: good little Catholic girl
wearing a neat blue uniform and my ordinary brown
    haircut
—one that made me look more like Sally Field in *The Flying
    Nun*
than Farrah Fawcett.
I was the daughter
who would enforce the daily afterschool parental "to do"

list.
If I couldn't get my sisters to do their jobs,
I did them myself.
I tried to be a good sister.
I'm still trying.

Meg
1979

Let's start on the morning that Maura went away to college. She was a year ahead of me in school and heading to Chestertown. I decided to be nice and make breakfast for everyone—eggs, bacon, toast, and sliced pineapple; the works. I put a little vodka in my OJ when no one was looking.

Maura is in a dreamy mood. My little sister Mia is crying fake tears, just to get attention. Mom is trying hard *not* to be teary, even though everyone knows Mom likes Maura better than any of the rest of us. Who else is going to listen to her mope about Dad? It's not going to be me, that's for damn sure. Dad is in his own little world as usual. No one will cooperate and just sit down and eat while it's hot.

"Everyone needs to sit. I got up early to cook," I told them, but did they listen? Of course not. The smell of eggs is making me feel a little sick, but I sit down and pretend to eat. I can't say I'm sorry to see Maura go. We sort of share a room. To appease us, our parents built a wall in the middle of our big room. Now, I'll be able to spread out and hang my clothes in Maura's closet. Maybe I'll even sleep in her bed.

Plus, I'm sort of pissed at Maura right now. I don't know why she needs to get into my business. Last night, she got nosy and started asking questions. Asking me if I got sick or if I'm okay. Asking me why it smells like puke in our bathroom. I don't have time to deal with her questions, so the timing's perfect for her to just get out of town.

Maura

Only Mom and I take the trip
to the Eastern Shore of Maryland
on my first day of college.
We drive in an old green sedan
with the windows open
because the car's air conditioning is broken.
Mom should have let me drive from the start.
She's afraid of the Bay Bridge.
As a child whenever she went to the beach,
she'd cover her eyes
and ask her brothers to tell her when they had crossed
over.

"Just keep talking to me like we're just driving on a normal
road," Mom says.
"It is a normal road, Mom. Don't worry. You could let me
drive."
"That would just make it worse.
I've got to learn to do this. It's ridiculous now
that I'm going to need to cross all the time
just to see you." She clenches the steering wheel.
Her breathing quickens, and she starts to sweat.
"Pull over, Mom. Let me drive across, and you won't even
have to look."
"I can do this, dammit."
I tell her, "I know you *can*, but you don't have to. Just pull
over here.
I'll get us across the bridge, and then you can go back to
driving once we're across."
"All right," she finally agrees. "I feel like shit, anyway."

We are back on the road,
with me at the wheel. We keep talking.
There are a million things on my mind,
but most of them don't have anything
to do with going away to college.
We pay at the tollbooth
and start the high climb up to the top of the bridge.
Blue sky and water,
with hundreds of sailboats leaning in the wind. I feel a
    thrill
from the expanse below us, not the fear
that grips my mother.
She has her head in her hands and she's coaching herself,
telling herself to breathe, telling herself we're almost
    there.
Don't look, she keeps saying, *don't look.*

I need to talk to her about Meg in the next hour
or the opportunity will be lost
until Thanksgiving. Last night's
fight with Meg still weighs on my mind. I know
I should do something, but I don't want to make things
    worse
by saying the wrong thing to Meg
or to Mom.

"Hey, Mom, we're across," I tell her hunched form
in the seat next to me. "You did great. Are you okay?"
"I wish it weren't nine in the morning. I need a drink."
"I want to talk to you about something, Mom, but I don't
    want you to overreact."

"Great. Now I *really* need a drink. What's wrong?"
"I had a conversation last night with Meg."
"Maybe we should pull over..."
"I'd really rather not stop. We're supposed to get to school
      before 10:00 am."
"Okay, Maura. Just say what you want to say."
"I'm worried about Meg."
"Why so?" Mom asks.
"Well, I don't know, but I think Meg might be sick
or something. I tried to talk to her about it,
but she wouldn't admit anything was wrong."
"What do you mean by *sick*?" Mom asks.
I hear the emotion escalating
in my mother's voice. I already regret
trying to bring this subject up.
"I've wanted to say something before,
but I wasn't sure about it
and I'm still not positive about it. It's just that sometimes
it's obvious
someone has gotten sick in our bathroom,
and last night, I could smell vomit and see that someone
had gotten sick in the toilet. When I asked,
Meg denied it
and started yelling at me when I asked her if she threw up.
Who else could have done it?
It wasn't me, and Mia would have said something."
"This just happened yesterday?"
"I've noticed things before, but I didn't know what to say.
It's not like she's easy
to talk to, you know.
I just have a feeling that something is wrong.
Our bathroom smells like, you know...

vomit. This sounds really disgusting to say aloud."
Mom waited, but then asked,
"Are you saying you think Meg has an eating disorder?"
"I think she might be bulimic. I think we should just keep
    an eye on her."
"Well, I guess since you'll be at school
for the next four years, you mean *I* should keep an eye on
    her."
My mom shakes her head. She's quiet for a while,
but finally, she says aloud,
"If it's not one damn thing, it's another with that girl."

Meg

Look, I might get in trouble more than the average girl, but why shouldn't I? It's my life and who else is going to live it? Things have gotten a little out of control lately. My boyfriend Mark is off to college and I'm left thinking about him all the time. Saying goodbye to him was one of the hardest things I've had to do. Even though he wasn't "Leavin' on a Jet Plane," he kept singing to me, "Kiss me and smile for me. Tell me that you'll wait for me. Hold me like you'll never let me go..." on our last night together. How can I help feeling rotten? He is my absolute soulmate—the one I'm meant to be with forever. Why does he have to go off to a school in freaking Virginia? Last year was perfect. I met Mark. I was writing for the school paper, attending football games, and hanging out with all my new friends. Last year, I'd be wearing my favorite blue T-shirt, the one with the beads sewn into the neckline and my favorite bell-bottom jeans, watching the clock, waiting for Mark to walk by my speech class in the middle of period 4. Then I'd get a pass from fat Mrs. Stover and we'd get to see each other for a few minutes. Get a drink from the water fountain. Pretend we were going to the library or the office. We'd make our way to one of our favorite spots.

"I was afraid Stover wouldn't sign my pass," I told Mark.

He grabbed my wrist and pulled me into the locker alcove.

"Just come here for a minute," he said, pulling me along to our secret corner.

I remember the adrenaline rush. Feeling how strong he was and maybe being in awe of him, but more than that, how I felt magnetically drawn to him.

I'd feel his strong arms holding me close, his hot breath on my neck. How quickly this could get spoiled— either by a teacher or some random person walking by.

It was such a rush, being with Mark. We got caught a couple of times in the alcove, and that meant detention and a letter home. Still it was worth all the risk. I lived to be with him. In detention, we'd just sit and stare at each other across the room. Mark came up with all sorts of silent silliness and I would giggle and the detention monitor, Ms. Murphy, would tell us to shush. She would never dismiss us both at the same time; usually she let me out first and I would wait on the bench near the parking lot for Mark. It took everything in me not to just run and leap on him when he came out of the door. I just sat there watching him swagger over to me until *zap*! It was an almost an electric jolt when he touched me.

It was like this my whole junior year and Mark's senior year of high school. It was one of those weird things where I didn't even know Mark existed until my best friend, Mindy, told me that he liked me. Because he was a year ahead—in Maura's year, I didn't have too many opportunities to be in class with him. When Mindy told me about him, I started looking for him in the cafeteria. I remember the first time I saw him, I couldn't really believe my eyes. The attraction was instantaneous. He was beyond any of my wildest dreams of handsome. To me, he looked like a California surfer with his blond hair and tanned skin, but he was smart, too.

Pretty soon after I first noticed him, we had chances to talk. Most of the conversations were lame on my part. We would "accidentally" both be walking out of the cafeteria at the same time and he would say hello and I would turn all red and hot in the face. At first, all I could really do in his presence was stare and smile and giggle. I would try to speak, but my words got all tangled. Fortunately for me, he had no such trouble. He didn't need much encouragement to talk. Words for him just spilled out.

"You know," he would say, "You're kinda cute. What do you say we just skip our classes and take a stroll?" He kept talking even though I was awestruck and couldn't think of anything to say. I wasn't even sure what he was talking about half the time. He never asked what I thought, so I could just gaze in amazement at his flawless face without ever really having to respond.

We would walk into the cafeteria and I'd be thinking how cool it was that everyone was seeing us together, and he'd say, "Dr. Ray's government class was so amazing today." I'd look up at him with big eyes, and he'd continue, "I got a great idea for a cartoon. It's going to be a caricature of Marvin Mandel with Democrats in one pocket and Republicans in the other." I would nod and smile and toss my head like he'd said the most hilarious thing ever.

Meeting him was the best thing that ever happened to me, or so I thought at the time. I have my best friend and neighbor, Mindy, to thank for that, but now he's going to UVA. He promises that I can come visit him. It will be fun to take a road trip to college if I can ever convince my parents to let me go.

Life has been dull and different since Maura went away to school, too. It's quieter anyway without her music playing nonstop. She likes Jackson Browne and plays his songs over and over until you just want to strangle her. Why can't she just wear headphones and not pollute the rest of the world with her depressing music?

I'm not sure what she said to Mom about my dieting habit. I know she said something because Mom has been hovering around my bathroom, and she never did that before. But hey, desperate times call for desperate measures. I'm not going to lose Mark to some college girl, and this works for me. If I eat too much, I just throw up. It's not like I do it all the time. Sometimes it's good enough to starve myself a little—just drink Diet Pepsi, eat a few cucumber slices. That's what feels the best. I get a kick out of not eating for a few days. Sometimes I'm forced to have dinner with my family, and Mom is a pain in the ass when it comes to cleaning your plate. She should stop eating everything on her plate, that's for sure!

The worst part is when Mom wants to *talk* about it. I don't see how it's anybody's business, and I am not like Maura. I do not want to sit and chat with Mom for hours on end. I have things to do, like go visit Mindy. Mom always wants to know everything—where I'm going, who I'll be with, when I'll be back. I don't see why I should have to explain everything. I'm not a baby anymore, and I don't need people in my business, which is one reason why I am furious at Maura. I wish I hadn't sent her my letter with my senior picture. I'm ready to send her another letter now, that's for sure, or to *never speak to her again*; I'm not sure which.

Last night as I was trying to sneak past Mom, as usual, Mom said, "Meg, come talk for a minute."

"I would, Mom, but Mindy's expecting me. We have to practice our French dialogue."

"This won't take long. Come in here for a second." When I go into our living room, I can see that she's got her typical end-of-the-day glass of Scotch.

"Can I have some of that?" I ask, pointing to the whiskey.

"I thought you were in a hurry to go study French."

"I've never tried studying French drunk before. You never know. Maybe it will help my grades."

"Stop joking around and come talk to me."

"Whatever, Mom. What do you want?"

"Well, if you're not even going to sit down, I'll just say it then. I signed you up for a six-week program on eating disorders at Immanuel Hospital," she blurts out.

I think maybe I'm hearing things. "Are you kidding me?" I scream.

"I've done some research, and I think you should go."

"Are you out of your mind? Is this all because of something Maura said, because she doesn't know what she's talking about!"

"Leave Maura out of this. She tried to talk to you, and you wouldn't have a civil conversation with her, so now I'm *telling* you. You will go to this program. I'll drive you downtown every Wednesday for six weeks."

"I cannot believe this!"

"Look, Meg. I've been reading about these eating disorders and they're nothing to mess with. Look at this article I just read," she says, shaking some magazine at me.

"Mom, I don't have to read any article. I think you must be drunk or something. Look, just because I'm the only person around here who isn't *obese* doesn't mean I have an eating disorder!"

"You can be mean if you want to, but you're signed up to go. The brochure is on the table there."

"Well, I'm not going, and you can't make me!"

"We'll see what your father has to say about this..."

"That is just about the lamest thing I've ever heard. You think *Dad* is going to send me away to some hospital?"

"Megan Elizabeth, your father and I love you very much. We've spent a lot of time discussing this. We are not sending you away, but eating disorders are dangerous. We've got to *do* something."

"You don't know anything, and I'm not going!" I leave the room and walk into the kitchen. There is a bowl of potatoes meant for Dad, but he can never manage to make it home in time for dinner. I take a bite of the cold mashed potatoes. They don't taste good, but I eat them all, and then I look for something to wash them down.

Maura

Hours away from home
and I still can't escape the drama.
Mom has written me
three letters this week.
I can picture the whole scene:
Mom sitting on the blue sofa—drinking
scotch in her little pewter cup,
trying to read, fuming,
scribbling her worries in letters to me.
Dad isn't home yet.
He likes to stop for a drink,
sometimes a long drink.
Mia is singing in her room
at the top of her lungs
using a hairbrush for a microphone.
Megan is hiding,
or sneaking out of the house to complain
to Mindy about how she hates all of us.
Mom signed Meg up
for an eating disorders program at Immanuel Hospital.
What a bombshell! Glad I missed that.
So now Mom has to drive Meg to Baltimore,
which scares her even more than the Bay Bridge.
Who would guess she'd act so soon?
When she told the people at Immanuel
our suspicions, they said,
"Sign her up right away."

The whole thing has driven a wedge
between Meg and me.

She says I betrayed her
and then, she tries to make a case
for her *dieting method.*
I tell her *I'm only trying to help,*
but she's too angry to listen. I don't know
how to fix any of this
and I don't really have time to think about it
if I want to pass my classes.

All that matters is getting help for Meg.
Am I right?
Anorexia and bulimia didn't sound as bad as
sexually transmitted diseases
when I first heard about them in health class,
but I'm scared. I don't want anything bad
to happen to my sister.

Meg

"I'm ready to run away from home. I'm serious. If I could think of a place to go, I would do it," I tell Mindy.

"Yeah, it really sucks, but believe me, you wouldn't like it any better at my house," Mindy says.

"They just don't understand at all and I can't explain it to them. There is nothing wrong with dieting this way," I continue.

"Well..." Mindy says, but she doesn't agree with me.

"Lots of people do worse things, like take laxatives. I wouldn't do that. Well, maybe I would try it once," I tell her. My feeling is this. I'm in control. It feels good, and for me, it's effective. If I eat too much—a burger and fries—I can just get rid of it. It's not a problem. I feel great. I look good in my clothes and Mark likes me this way.

Mindy is such a good listener, and she's so much fun. We like to sit on the back seat of the bus and rate the people when they get on. Their outfits and things. If they are worth noticing. She always says the funniest things and gets me laughing so hard I nearly fall off the seat. We got mad at each other last year for a while, and I didn't speak to her for like three months, but then we made up and it's been great ever since. I think she said something mean about Mia that got me mad. After all, Mia can't help who she is. Mia's annoying, but still. I can't even remember what Mindy said, but sometimes her harsh comments aren't too funny if they're directed at you or your little sister.

My mother had German measles when she was pregnant with Mia. That's as close to a reason as we ever got for why Mia is the way she is. It's fair to say she's a challenge. My dad sold the tree business he inherited from his dad to take a job helping people with disabilities. He had a dream that he could start a horticulture and landscaping business run predominantly by workers with handicaps. He had a dream that he could help his youngest daughter find some happiness the way he had, by planting trees and flowers.

But Mia is Mia, and so far, she isn't interested in flowers or working with people who are *handicapped* or doing anything people tell her to do. Mia is interested in three things: kittens, boys, and cars. She loves the feeling of a kitten in her fingers, even if that kitten is biting or hissing with bared teeth. She's brave like that. She loves the soft ears, the gentle purr, and the wildness of kittens. She also loves boys and cars. Come to think of it, maybe that's why I have a sweet spot for her, because I am a sucker for boys and cars, too. When you meet Mia, you have to be impressed by her determination. She won't let anything stop her when she sets her mind on something. Half the time I'm embarrassed and annoyed by her and the other half, I just look at her and think there is no one else in the world like her.

Maura

At eleven years old, I became exactly
the person I am today—
the one who writes poems
and likes to cook.
Mom would leave a recipe and a note
that said, "Make this for dinner."
I remember a chicken
brown on the outside,
frozen on the inside.
It's probably a miracle that I didn't
burn down the house or poison anyone.
But I made my first apple pie this way,
and I'm glad to have cooking skills now,
even though at the time, I felt the unfairness
that I had to be the one to cook dinner
when Meg would be playing softball
and I would be the one in the kitchen
trying to figure out the difference between
sliced and diced onions.

We weren't always a total shipwreck of a family.
We used to laugh and take ordinary beach vacations.
Lately, though, there's not too much laughter.
I don't know the whole story of why
Dad is out of the house so much.
When we are all together in the house, there is usually
some fight brewing and Dad is a lover, not a fighter.
Meg and I can't have a conversation
that doesn't end in a fight, at least that's the way it seems.
She doesn't understand why I want to read and write

and I don't understand why she spends so much time
fixing her hair and talking on the phone.
I turn up the music so I don't have to listen to her
    conversations,
  and she screams through the wall for me to turn down
    the music.
All this is normal sister stuff, I guess,
but what happens if I really need to talk to her?
Why is *yelling* the only way she ever talks to me?

My college roommate, JoAnn,
is using some kind of brown diet powder
for weight loss, and she offered me some.
It's supposed to taste like chocolate.
It wouldn't hurt if I lost a few pounds.
I tried beer for the first time
on my first day in Chestertown. It made me feel dizzy
and I needed to lie down at 4:00 in the afternoon.
JoAnn laughed at me for that.
The meals they serve in the cafeteria
are all super-caloric—broccoli and cheese casserole,
lots of potatoes. I should be more careful.
There is just so much food to choose from and I find myself
    not
making very good choices. The whole cafeteria scene is
    stressful.
I don't like to go in there by myself, so I try to find people
to go with, but that means I have to stop reading
or waste time trying to figure out
who I can sit with in the dining hall. JoAnn tolerates me,
but we aren't really friends.

Mom isn't helping with my diet plans.
I got a little slip in my mailbox that said I had a package,
and the package turned out to be
Mom's buttery, homemade chocolate chip cookies.

Meg

I'm not sure what to do. I was planning a trip to Charlottesville to visit Mark. At first, he was putting me off, saying things like he had to change plans because of football and tough classes. He couldn't come home, but he knew a girl named Laurel that I could stay with who was in his study group. Telling me he missed my cuddly little self. But then yesterday, I got this letter in the mail. I had started a habit of waiting on the front porch for the mailman. I was so excited when I saw the letter. I held it in my hands and ran back to the swing on the front porch to read it with no one around.

October 2, 1979

Dear Meg,

This is a hard letter to write. I wish I didn't have to write it, but I've always been honest with you, and truthfully, I don't know how else to be. You are going through some hard things right now and I'm sorry that I'm not home to be a friend to you. It's only been a brief time, but I am totally immersed in my life here. I know I should write to you and come home to see you, but I just can't tear myself away from all that I've got going on. I think you will understand when you go away next year. It just totally absorbs your energy, time, and attention.

For all these reasons and probably more that I'll share when we talk, I think we should take a breather from our boyfriend/girlfriend status. We each need to focus on our own separate issues now and get our heads on straight, if you know what I mean. I don't know exactly how many miles we are from each other literally, but I feel like I'm living on the moon and you are living in a galaxy beyond. What can I say? What can I do? High school, my hometown, and even my beautiful gal pal all seem like distant dreams that were once real but exist no longer.

I can't promise that I am making any sense, but please know that I am not doing this to hurt you. I really believe that this will help you, too, in the long run. You have serious things going on with the counseling that need your full attention. I'm just an unnecessary distraction in this scenario. And it's not fair to lead you to believe that I am the same guy I was a few short months ago. Things have changed and I am a changed man. We will discuss this. I want you to understand. I want you to know that I am not taking this lightly. I would never intentionally hurt you. You must know this after all we have meant to each other.

Love Always,
Mark

As I sat on the porch, all the other mail fell to the ground and started blowing away. I couldn't believe this was happening. I had to read it twice before shock turned to anger which turned to disbelief which turned to determination to fix everything that was broken. No, this was not going to happen. No way.

When I read the letter to Mindy, she just called him an arrogant jerk. She wanted to know where he came up with lines like "take a breather from our boyfriend/girlfriend status." She said I was better off without him. Should I remind her that she's the one who introduced us? My response is different though. All I can think of is *how can I get down there*? If I see him, I can get him to change his mind.

Maura

I can see Meg and Mark together
with matching tans and bleached hair--
the perfect couple.
It's too much
all at once. How could he
do this to her?

I admit I've been jealous
watching how easy they laugh
at dumb things. How even sharing
a bowl of ice cream could keep them
entertained for an hour. As if being in love
could make everything sweet and hilarious.

How could he dump her so fast? When
they had a five-year plan that involved
degrees and journalism and *New Yorker* cartoons
and a flat in Manhattan where you could drink
Bloody Marys on a Sunday morning
in your PJs.

Meg

I can't believe I have to go to this stupid group counseling session tonight. I was quiet on the way down to Immanuel Hospital and back home again. Down the JFX with the slow traffic and Mom's occasional use of the f-word when someone cuts her off. I'm just going through the motions with this counseling thing, and the only thing on my mind is *how do I get Mark back?*

I know if I can just see him, I can change things around. I have the power of persuasion, and we just had the best summer of our lives working together at the pool. And we had our famous speedy road trip to Ocean City on a day in July. We fed one French fry to a seagull and then they dive bombed us and the fries scattered everywhere. We napped on the beach and cooled off in the waves and got back home around midnight.

Maybe I can go to UVA instead of Randolph Macon. There's no reason to break up just because we can't see each other every day. I can get my way about this. I know I can.

My counselor's name is Teresa, and she always has this big-toothed grin that I would like to slap right off her face.

Last week's session was about healthy food choices. Really? I'm going through the motions to get Mom off my back, but this whole thing is so lame. I am meeting interesting people though. First and foremost is this woman named Ruth, who I know must be Ruth Carson of the *Sunpapers*, even though we don't use last names in the group. I recognized her right away from the picture next to her column in the paper. As a writer for my school paper, I've always seen her as a role model. She's obviously a bunch older than me but she has the life I want. She's a famous journalist with a good job. Her column is sharp and focused on relevant things people care about. I wanted to tell her that in group, but it wasn't the right time. Still, it was profound that she was in my group. Seeing her there made me feel almost proud of my eating 'problems,' like somehow we're members of this elite club of women on the move--women who don't need food to survive.

Not that there aren't some losers in our group, but for the most part, you wouldn't know that any of us had a *problem*. We just care about our appearances is all, and we don't want to turn into fat blobs like so many people who shouldn't even go into public looking the way they do.

Just a few more weeks of the eating disorders group to go, and then Teresa can take a hike. Mom's already trying to rope me in to more counseling, but I'm not going to do it. My priority now is getting Mark back.

Mom says, "You'll meet somebody new."

Dad says, "I never liked that pompous ass anyway."

Mia says, "My boyfriend Ronny has a brother."

But I don't care what anyone says. I'm not giving up on Mark.

Maura

I save Mom's letters
in a zippered pouch. The latest one
tells of a truce with Meg
and how everyone in the house
tiptoes gingerly
around her, checking her mood
before speaking,
avoiding subjects that might
set her off.

Mom's always waiting for
Dad to come home.
There are things to be done
around the old house:
a leak in the basement,
a mouse in the kitchen.

Dad wants a cold one
and some time to trim the boxwood topiary.
Mom wants him to deal with the leak
or the teenage daughter who needs the most attention.

I'm glad I miss the family meetings
that end in tears with Mom yelling
and Meg yelling
and Mia biting her arm in frustration.
Poor Dad!
No wonder he has trouble
finding a road
to bring him home

in time for supper.

Hours away, I just hope
to pass my mid-term exams.

I have a quiet cubby in the library
that overlooks a brick terrace
and a mountain of reading for Cultural Anthropology
and a poem due in Creative Writing.

Meg

I have a love/hate relationship with my mirror. I aim for Farrah Fawcett curls and on a good hair day, I feel great. So shoot me, I like fashion—nice clothes, stylish hair, and jewelry. I just wish I could like what I see in the mirror more often or that I could just stop looking.

Sometimes I get teased for trying on too many outfits. Should I wear pink or should I wear blue? Color is the thing. Blue eye shadow and a tube top. Or a classy bold red? Bright yellow can work with a pendant and hoops. Mom has lots of scarves, but I can never get them to work just right. It's so much fun to play with possibilities, but of course, it all finally depends on if I can get my hair to work with the blow dryer and the curling iron.

In my room, my outfit looks put together, my hair looks fine, but by the time I get to school, who knows? Will my makeup still look okay? What will the other girls think?

And then, there are the fatal flaws. Things I was born with and can't change. It's my butt that's worried me the most. Mom and I have a lot in common: the same bone structure, the same tiny hands and wrists, and I'm afraid to say—the same big rear end! The rest of me can look okay, presentable, but I can't think of one time I've looked in a full-length mirror and thought *damn my butt looks good*.

I do squats and lunges every day trying to reduce and tone! It doesn't help that hip huggers with bell bottoms are in right now. I bought a pair of orange hip huggers. The tag said Burnt Sienna. I loved those pants and thought they looked good with the lemon body suit, but the first time I wore them, Mark took one look and said, "Girl, you have a big ass, and I'm not talking donkeys." I let him have his joke, but I never wore those pants again.

The other problem area—my teeth. Our dentist recommended braces because a couple of my front teeth are crooked, but because it was going to cost thousands of dollars, my parents said no. I can't believe they wouldn't do what the dentist suggested. For sure you can bet if Maura or Mia needed braces, they wouldn't even have questioned it!

The mirror has power over me and so does the scale. I'm constantly trying to keep my weight in a good range. It's been harder since the breakup letter. I eat too much and then get disgusted with myself. After that, it's either starve myself or get rid of the food I've already eaten.

I get this great feeling if I just stop eating for a few days. I like being able to feel my bones. It's not really a problem for me, but if I eat too much, my body automatically wants to get rid of it a few minutes later.

Mindy and I have been going to Friendly's for junk food lately—burgers on toast and wrinkly fries. Mom and Dad have been feeling sorry for me and letting me do whatever I want. They like it when I eat. I guess that makes them think I'm "normal." And I have to keep up my appearances. Everybody thinks I'm a pathetic loser because of the famous Dear Jane letter, but I'll show all of them. Mark and I will be back together by Christmas.

In Friendly's last night there were a bunch of people from school. There was one guy who kept staring at me. He was thin and had curly brown hair. I asked Mindy if she knew him. "Yeah, that's Larry Stone. He's a senior, too," she told me. "He's smart and runs track."

"Hey, that works. Introduce me, and I'll interview him for the *Pipeline*," I said.

"I don't know him that well. He won't even know who I am," Mindy said, giving me her trademark little shake of the head and eye roll.

"Be that way," I told her. "I'll introduce myself." So, I marched right over to the booth where he was sitting before I could think about it too much. He was there with three other guys, and I didn't know any of them. On the table was a massive pile of food and all of them except Larry were diving in. "Are you Larry Stone, the track star?" I asked. "I write for the *Pipeline*, and I was hoping you might give me an interview, after you finish eating, of course. I'm sitting over there with my friend, Mindy."

Larry just sat there for several long seconds, and I didn't think he was going to reply. One of the other guys at the table spoke up. "We're all on the team. If genius here won't talk to you, I will. I'm Skip McCall, and I'm *really* the star of the team." The others started throwing fries at Skip. He just laughed and said, "Thanks for the fries, men."

"Well, I'm over here with my notebook, if you decide you want some press," I said. Larry kept staring but still didn't say a word. As I walked away, I heard all of them laugh. I hoped they weren't laughing about my butt.

Maura

When I have a poem that's due,
I head down to the town dock
to look at the water.
I love the old brick sidewalks
and the historic buildings.
My mind relaxes and I can breathe.
It's strange to me
that instead of writing
about the beauty of the Chester River at dawn,
I end up always writing about home.
I wonder what my mother is doing,
and I picture her in the kitchen.
In this poem, I imagine her thinking about her wedding
anniversary.

The Vow

Gingham waves at the window
as humidity
stirs the early kitchen quiet.

Coffee spills to the cup.
She grips the hot blackness.
It is a cold June.

He sleeps, dull with consequence,
while she looks to the garden
crystallized by mist.

Blameless in the first light

green and silver limbs
sprawl in idle elegance

asserting their purpose.
She wipes a tear,
but the stain remains.

Tongue-tied knots
hold longer than marriage
and Catholic promises.

When did they strike
the match? When did
they snuff the flame?

She carries now an empty cup,
expecting the justice of pain
to rouse her each morning.

Meg

Did I learn anything from the forced participation in the six-week program for eating disorders at Immanuel Hospital? Not really. I can't remember the first time I ever threw up my dinner, but I do remember the first time my sister Maura "caught" me. I remember feeling so superior to her in that moment. I was the thin one, and she was the lard-ass who didn't know anything.

I do realize there are risks with dieting this way, but I have things under control. It's hard to look good, but it's worth it. If I don't work at it, I'll end up looking like all the other porkers in my family.

Food is a big part of what we've always done as a family. We had jelly doughnuts after church and then we'd go out to brunch at the Sheraton Hotel when we were kids. My sisters and I were allowed to run ahead on the green carpet. I was always first—the fastest by far, then my sister, Mia, the hyper one, and last of all, Maura, who runs like a cow.

The lure of the buffet was mesmerizing. I took my time to study the choices: the warm and cold food, the tiny muffins, the neat boxes of cereal. I could drink fresh-squeezed orange juice and eat whatever I wanted.

No one fought me, no one told me what to eat, and we all got along for the whole glorious day. I had a feeling then that my choices had no consequences. I could eat sticky buns and bacon, pancakes and fresh pineapple. I just filled up on all the good things.

Contrast that with my mother making me sit at the dining room table after everyone else was excused because I didn't eat my peas. I hate peas, and there was no way I was going to eat them. I think I finally squished the waxy things in my napkin. They were cold and stinky sweet, and it makes me sick now just to think about it.

My mom used to laugh and tell the story about how, when she was pregnant, her doctor would get mad at her if she gained too much weight from her last appointment. Her solution was to starve herself before the appointment and then go buy a dozen doughnuts afterward and eat the whole box. Then she'd begin the whole starvation thing again before her next doctor visit. And she thinks she can lecture me about my dieting? Because of her, I started bingeing before I was even born.

Now, I'm an honest person, but my thoughts and feelings about food stayed secret. People don't want to hear the truth about any of this. If I were a smoker, like Dad, there would be little licorice candies to help me quit. In the group, they kept saying that people with eating disorders have trouble managing their emotions in a healthy way, but I am managing my emotions just fine. It's not a problem for me.

What is a problem is how Mom just mopes around the house since Maura's gone to college. Mom just wallows in sadness—reading William Butler Yeats and drinking too much scotch in her little pewter cup. Because Maura's in a poetry class, Mom is trying to write a poem about Nana. She looks like she's in tears all the time, which is just so awkward. What am I supposed to do about her constant depression? She wants *me* to go to counseling, but *she's* the one who needs it.

So, I pretend I'm getting better to cheer things up around the house. I tell Mom *I learned my lesson. I'm not throwing up anymore. Hallelujah!*

Last night, at the end of our last group meeting, Teresa gave us a brochure with phone numbers and told us to call if we need anything.

Driving home in the rain, Mom asked, "Do we need to call a private counselor to help you get through this, Meg?"

"Help me get through what?"

"Don't be difficult, Meg. You know what I'm saying. Do you want to keep seeing someone who knows about eating disorders? I didn't get the feeling that Teresa was all that qualified."

"I don't need any help, Mom. I just need everyone to leave me alone."

"Okay," Mom said, sounding defeated. "I just want you to tell me if we need to do more. I can't read your mind."

"Whatever, Mom. Could we just not talk anymore? I brought my calculus notes. I want to study for my quiz tomorrow."

"Well, you do need to work on that grade," Mom agreed.

So that's how that conversation ended, with me being a badass, shutting my mother out.

Maura

"Hey, Meg, do you think
you could get your stuff
off my bed?" There are hot
curlers and scarves and wet
towels flung everywhere.

"Meg!" I say, again.

"On the phone!" she yells back
through the wall that sort of
separates our room.

So much for coming home
to a peaceful family Thanksgiving.
I have two papers due next week,
a poem to write for workshop
and mountains of reading. My jeans
are already tight and I haven't eaten
one bite of turkey or pumpkin pie.

I grab Meg's stuff
and dump it on her bed.
I'm glad she's on the phone
or we'd already be fighting.
Instead, she just gives me a dirty look.

The only thing
she's said to me since I've been home:
"There's the college girl
wearing her freshman fifteen."

I start to wonder
when we'll have dinner.
Wafting through the house
I smell the sweet and sour
of cranberry and sauerkraut.

In the kitchen
Mia is chirping about a boy from Bible study
and Dad is talking about *why don't we all
take a little trip somewhere?*
and Mom is peppering me with questions
I only halfway hear and only halfway want to answer.
The kitchen is cramped and tiny;
every bit of counter space is cluttered
with things like homemade pie
or warm corn pudding.
Mom's using a potato masher
with great force. "Set the table,"
she says. Mom doesn't look as stressed
as she sounds in her letters.
It smells incredible in here.
"Look at this turkey," she says,
opening the oven door. "We got it
from Uncle Tom's Farm."
"I thought you said you were going
to keep things simple," I say.
"I just got inspired—with you coming home
and all of us together for a meal for a change."
She keeps mashing the potatoes. "While you are home,
keep an eye on your sister. I think she's up
to her old tricks." I reach for the stainless steel.

Mom says, "Let's use the good silver. I'm not asking
you to spy on her, but just let me know if you notice
anything." I say, "Even if I do notice anything
what can we do? Did you hear that crack she made
about my weight?" Mom says, "God knows, she's not
an easy person, but she's had a hard time of it. I can't
    believe
Mark dropped her just like that after all the time
they'd been together."

"Was the program at Immanuel good for her?" I ask.
"She said it was, but I have my suspicions that it's all
    started up again.
Food will go missing that I was sure we had. She eats after
    we go to bed,
and she and Mindy go out a lot. Drinking might be
    involved there.
Just let me know if you see anything."
"Maura, the secret agent? I don't think so, Mom."

Thanksgiving dinner goes like this:
after *maybe* the first bite, Meg says,
"So, Dad, after dinner,
do you think I could go to this party
over in Bowley's Quarters?"
Mia says, "Can I go, too?"
Dad says to Meg, "Pass me the potatoes, sweetie."
Mom says, "Can't we just enjoy this one meal together,
    Meg?
Where the hell is Bowley's Quarters, anyway?"
I say, "Everything's delicious, Mom."
"It's not too far. It's in Baltimore County. Larry is driving,
and he's a safe driver," says Meg.

Mia says, "Larry's really cute."

"Does everyone have enough to eat?" says Mom,

trying to stay cheerful. "I won't be out late," Meg

continues. Mom's tone changes, "Drop it, Meg,

it's Thanksgiving. Or the answer's no, if you can't drop it
     now."

"I don't know what the big deal is," says Meg. "I'm just
     making

pleasant dinner conversation. Please pass the corn."

From that point on

you could hear the sound

of silver forks hitting china.

I could see the blue and pink birds on my plate.

So, I took more stuffing and potatoes because they were
     right

in front of me. I would have had more turkey, but I didn't
     want

to have to ask someone to pass it to me.

Meg

I have got to get the hell out of Boring, Maryland! It was fine when I was little and we could walk to the General Store and post office, and it's okay if you like rolling hills and fields of green, that sort of thing, but we are in the middle of freaking nowhere!

I want to live in a snazzy condo or a brownstone in New York City, a place where I can wear my good shoes and hear the way they sound on the sidewalk. I want to live in a place where style is appreciated, and the pace is brisk.

I don't know what I'd do if Mindy weren't across the street. Last week, she was over, and we were just hanging out when we decided we should have the guys over for dinner—Larry and Mindy's boyfriend, Kevin. Dad and Mom and Mia had left earlier for the Eastern Shore. They were all headed to Washington College to visit Maura, so I wouldn't have to deal with them for the whole day!

Larry and I are officially a couple. We kissed at the party in Bowley's Quarters. The house there was huge, with enormous glass windows so you could see the water from every room. I don't even know whose house it was. Somebody from the track team invited Larry, and he invited me. No parents anywhere in sight, which is how I like it. It sounded like Larry was as glad to escape his Thanksgiving dinner as I was to leave mine.

We had a great time, even though he is so NOT like Mark. He's kind of shy, and he reminds me a little of my dad with his big puppy eyes and his sandy brown curls. I can forget Mark for a little while when I'm with him. He's easygoing; not much rattles him. It's weird that he's so quiet. With Mark, I could hardly get a word in, but with Larry, I need to be the one to keep the conversation going. That is unless I bring up the subject of movies. Larry's got lots to say about *The Godfather* movies and films in general. He's helping me pass calculus, and that makes my parents like him better than Mark, which irks me a little. Still, with Larry, Mom doesn't fight me so much, and that's a good thing. He comes over to study and eat dinner. I go to his track events; track meets are so much *less fun* than watching Mark play football! Frankly, the track meets are long and dull. I have to spend too much time alone, and then at the end, he's all sweaty. Still, I like him, and I like having him like me.

With my family on the way to the Eastern Shore, the plans for our dinner party start to take shape. It's easy for Mindy to get permission to eat at my house. Nobody needed to know that my parents weren't going to be home! Mindy and I scrounge around for dinner ingredients. She makes a salad. We have a loaf of garlic bread in the freezer. It's just a matter of spicing up a jar of marinara sauce and cooking spaghetti and inviting the guys to come over.

We spend some time getting the food ready, but we spend more time getting ourselves ready. We raid the liquor cabinet and find sherry and Irish Mist. I wouldn't dare drink Mom's precious Scotch. We leave that alone— it's nasty anyway. We drink some of the sherry, which neither of us like, and then we drink the Irish Mist, which tastes better than the sherry. Then we take showers and paint our toes and then our fingernails. Mindy picks pink nail polish and I pick red. We end up trading outfits and it's so much fun.

By the time Larry and Kevin show up, we are pretty much toasted. We set the table in the dining room. We light a candle and the whole room sparkles. Larry brought wine—when he asked, that's what I told him we needed, and Kevin brought beer. None of us are old enough to drink legally, which is so lame.

We serve the food and have a real double date. Larry and Kevin don't know each other that well and neither of them have much to say, so the conversation doesn't exactly flow, but the boys eat the food and say it's good. I start to wonder when Mom and Dad will be home, but the idea is just floating around in the back of my mind. I'm not worried. I feel like a grown-up.

Mindy can't get home late without having to explain things to her mom, so she and Kevin leave about 10 o'clock. That leaves Larry and me alone in my house for the first time ever. After eating so much, I start to feel sick, and I get upstairs just in the nick of time. I tell Larry I'll be right back as I run up the stairs. It takes a while to take care of my business and brush my teeth. I'm surprised when I open the bathroom door and find Larry in the hallway.

"I hope you don't mind that I came up here. It's such a great old house. I love these steps," he says.

I laugh and say, "I think that's the most I've ever heard you say."

"This has been fun," he says, "but I need to head home."

"Don't go yet," I say. "Here, let me show you my room." We walk into the colossal mess that Mindy and I made with our beauty regimen. "Sorry about all this," I say moving the hair dryer and some wet towels. I make a place for him to sit down on the bed. He has a strange sort of scared look on his face, but he does sit. "I wish you could stay all night, but my family will be back at some point."

"Ahh, no," he says. "I couldn't stay. I didn't tell my mom when I'd be back, but we have a rule where I have to call if I won't be home by midnight."

"We have plenty of time then," I say.

"Well, then. Okay, then," he says, and I sit down on the bed next to him. We look awkwardly at each other for a few long seconds before he leans over and kisses me. It is one of those sweet little kisses, and I hope I taste like toothpaste. He kisses me again, and I kiss him back. All the heat in the room floods me, and I melt like chocolate. I feel his lean muscles, and I almost call him Mark. Almost. Thank God, I don't do that. We keep making out in a sort of time warp bubble until I hear the first pop of stones in the driveway.

"Shit!" I tell him. "They're home."

Maura

This weekend I'm overdosing
on parental involvement.
First, the surprise visit yesterday.
I didn't see my cute pixie sister
running toward me on the library terrace.
Instead, I saw Ellie May Clampett
of *The Beverly Hillbillies,*
coming straight at me,
hollering my name.

There is no hiding.
My secret is out.

My friend Will and I are walking up
from the Alumni House Saturday service
and there they are:
Mia, my dad, my mom.
"Maura, my big sista!" Mia yells.
I look around to see
who else sees them. It's bad enough
that Will has to witness this.
We are friends from crew and
both attend Saturday mass here on campus.

When I recover from the shock of seeing them, I say,
"Hey. What a surprise," while I'm thinking
what a nightmare, what a horror show,
when are you leaving? Mom starts rambling,
"Well, honey, you know your dad
when he gets it in his head that he wants to take a drive.

We're sorry for not letting you know
ahead of time. We've been wandering around
looking for you all day. We left a note on your dorm
room door." I think of all the people they've seen,
all the people they've talked to and my face reddens.

As if this isn't enough
Mia then asks Will, "Are you Maura's
boyfriend?" And my humiliation is complete.
I'm sure my face has darkened to purple, but I ignore
Mia and say to Mom and Dad,
"This is Will. I know I've told you about him.
We rode home together at Thanksgiving."
There is a shaking of hands and Mia giggles and asks Will,
"Do you have a girlfriend? I think you're cute!"
Mom says, "Leave Maura's friend alone, Mia."
Will's not sure how to play this, God help him,
but he gives her a little hug and says, "You're a real
cutie, yourself. Nice to meet you all, but I'm heading
off to dinner now."
"Why don't you join us for dinner?" Dad asks,
"No sir, I can't, but thanks," Will says.

As he walks away, Mia is practically
shouting, "Come back, Will. Don't you want my number?
Mom, what's my number?"

As soon as he's gone, I say,
"Mom, I've never been so embarrassed in my entire life!
Mia, why do you have to act like that?"
Mia says, "What did I do? I like your friend, Will. Do you
    think

he likes me?"

We drive to Fisherman's Wharf, but it's too crowded
so we end up having pizza. I'm furious at them
and at myself and the service is slow so by the time
they leave Chestertown, I am done. I try to read
for a while but end up just going with a crowd to a frat
party where I drink too much red punch
and get a screaming headache. It's bad
enough that my Saturday gets ruined but on Sunday
Mom makes her usual call at 3 p.m.
She's steaming over what they found
when they got home last night. Meg in her bedroom,
not alone, not fully dressed. Larry's car in the driveway
and a mess in the kitchen. Dirty dishes,
beer bottles, and spaghetti sauce on her white tablecloth.
Meg is grounded indefinitely.

Meg

Mom is on the warpath over a few dirty dishes. She needs to get a life. Usually Dad's the only one who can get her this mad.

I'm grounded, but that won't last. I hope I didn't get Mindy in trouble too by saying she was over here.

I don't care, though. It was so worth it. What's the big deal about having some friends over for dinner? I really don't get why they are both so angry. Dad scared Larry. He scared me, too. It's weird to have them both so upset. From the way they reacted, you would have thought I robbed a bank or committed murder. Mom keeps saying that I didn't ask permission. I just don't get it. *If I think they are going to trust me now, I have another thing coming!* On and on she drones, as if I'm listening, as if I give a shit.

I'm not feeling so good today. I'm probably a little hungover. Best if I just stay in my room.

Maura

December 27th and I'm home
on winter break. Meg is supposedly grounded
but if Mom and Dad aren't here
neither is Meg and I'm not
getting in the middle of it.

Joe, love of my life,
and manager of the pool where I work,
called to invite me
to a party. There will be
people I worked with at the pool
last summer and they are all older than me
by a few years
but I guess I'll go
if it's okay with Mom and Dad.

I've had this crush on Joe
for two summers.
He's 23 and so grown up
and serious about lifeguarding.
I like that he's five years older
than me and acts like a man, not a boy.
I learned the hard way
that things at a pool can change
so quickly. A high school
football player came for a swim
after practice one ordinary afternoon
and died. He was only seventeen.
He went to a private school.
I didn't know him.

Later, they said he'd had a heart attack
and we'd done CPR and that was all
we could do, but it wasn't enough to save him.

I was in the chair at the time,
but I didn't know what to do. I just blew the whistle
and stood there paralyzed. Joe was born
for moments like this and he took charge
and gave orders
and that's when I think I fell in love with him
or maybe it was later
when he comforted me
and answered everyone's questions
and told me it wasn't my fault.

Asking Mom for permission
to go to a party
can be tricky so I wait, and she wants to know
Who is Joe? Who is Gina?
And *where is the party going to be?*
And *aren't they all older than you?*
But eventually she says yes
and Meg and Mia are amazed that—yes!
I am finally going somewhere on a Saturday night.

Meg can't resist the urge to try
to do something with my hair
or tell me Joe is fat
and too old
and probably a pothead.
I stand to leave but she says,
"Sit, I'm not finished yet."

as the blow dryer ends yet another of our conversations.

The party is too small.
There are only seven people in the room,
and I am awkward
and out of place and
the only one who is still a teenager at 18
and I only know two of the seven people
and Joe and Gina don't really like each other.
So why am I here?
It feels like my conversational French class
where I don't know what to say
or how to say it.
I'm holding a warm bottle of beer,
taking careful sips.
I promised Mom I would not drink.
I lose track of time watching Joe
smoke a cigar
and listening to him talk about life as an EMT
and next year at the pool
and how his night classes are going.
Gina and her boyfriend leave.
Joe's brother Lee and his friends go off to the basement
and Joe and I are alone with a cat on the scratchy couch.

That's when I should have gone home.

The Schaefer beer puts a dull spell
on my senses. I feel unable to do anything but
accept the approaching moves toward me.
Joe's arm around my shoulders. His whiskered lips
brushing against my throat.

It doesn't occur to me to say no.
Why would I say no?

Someone told me later that it was 2 a.m.
when Dad banged on Joe's door.
Maybe I should feel embarrassed about that
but I just feel numb.
I tell Dad at the door,
"I'm fine, Dad. I just lost
track of time. I'm coming home now."

Meg

I really should remember to thank Maura sometime for the big distraction she caused over Christmas break. For once, I wasn't the only one being yelled at for doing normal things like staying out too late, drinking beer, etc. I can't really talk to her about it right now, but I'll have to tell her someday.

Larry was here because even though I'm grounded, he's still allowed to come over to watch a movie with me. It was about 11:30 p.m., and he was getting ready to leave so he could make his curfew, and Mom was a nervous wreck.

"Shouldn't Maura be home by now?" Mom said for the hundredth time. "I didn't tell her an exact time to be home, but shouldn't she be home already?" Dad was snoring on the La-Z-Boy, and Mom was wound like a top.

I couldn't help it; I started to laugh. And it was mean, but I started to say things like, "Maybe we should call the police or the fire department or the National Guard!" The whole scene was humorous; I couldn't help myself. I settled myself down and said, "In all seriousness, Mom. Maura's in college now. She probably stays out till three in the morning every night. Nothing's wrong with her. I'm sure of it."

Mom replied, "How can your father sleep at a time like this? Hal, wake up!"

"Mom, don't be ridiculous. Let him sleep. What's he going to do, anyway?"

"Hal! Hal!" she continued.

As much as Larry and I were enjoying this turn of events, he had to go, so I walked out with him. It was a cold night, and there were some magical snowflakes falling from a dark sky. I stuck my tongue out to taste them, and I grabbed Larry and kissed him in this giddy sort of mood.

"I wish you could stay, or I could go with you," I told him.

"You better let me go, though. My mom can be just like your mom, especially if there's snow in the forecast," Larry said.

"This snow isn't scary. Look how beautiful it is!"

"It is nice. Now let me go," he said, kissing me again.

"You must not really want to go," I said kissing back.

"Don't *want* to, have to," he said, breaking away, "I'll call you tomorrow."

By the time I go back in, I'm shivering, and Mom sees the snow on my jacket.

"Oh God, Hal. It's snowing!" Mom said.

Dad barely grunted an answer, but he was awake.

As I went up the stairs, I yelled, "Good night, you two! Maura is fine. Go to bed!"

Maura

Mom gave me a white leather journal
for Christmas. My only rule:
I write the date before I write, but I don't
have to write every day. I just have to
keep writing.
So far though, I want to write
because so much has happened, is happening.

My mother is freaking out. At first
it was just my staying out late
but then when I told her what happened
between Joe and me
she lost it—*You did what? You did what?*
And I guess I should have known it was dumb
to tell her
but we've always shared everything
so it never occurred to me
not to tell.

They always say
the first time is supposed to be painful
but the pain for me came afterward,
when he didn't call.

And then more pain, when he did call—
Mia picked up the phone and in her big voice yelled,
"Hullo! Who's this? Joe. Uncle Joe?"
I'm mouthing, *"Give me the phone!"*
and she's shooing me away with her left hand.
She keeps listening and finally says, "Okay. She's here."

"Hi," I say, "I'm glad you called." I drag the phone cord
as far as I can from my listening family.
Joe says, "Hello. I didn't want
to call right away. Your father seemed... angry."
I tell him, "That's not a problem," and ask,
"How are you?"
He says, "Well, I'm fine. Are you getting ready
to go back to school?"
"I go back tomorrow," I say,
"but I could meet you somewhere tonight."
"Look, Maura. I don't want you to get the wrong idea
about the other night," he says. I stay silent.
"There's a pretty big gap between our ages," he says.
"Five years," I say, as I'm thinking that my parents
are nine years apart.
"Five years doesn't seem
like much," he says, "but you're heading back
to school and it doesn't make much sense for us
to get too involved. I mean, I think you are a great girl
and all—very sweet."
"I understand what you're saying, but..." I try.
"Your parents wouldn't be too happy about me..." he says.
"Could we leave them out of this? It's not their business,"
    I say.
"But they could make it their business. You're young. They
    could
give me a hard time," he says.
"They wouldn't," I say.
"I've thought this through, and I don't see it working," he
    says.

He's always so sure of himself.

"I'm sorry," he says.
"I'm sorry, too," I say, choking back
the emotions bubbling to the surface.
"Joe, why do we have to say *right now*
that this for sure isn't going to work? I mean,
can't we wait until next summer to see what happens?"
"It's no use, Maura. Really," he says.
"Okay, then," I say. "I'm glad you called. I was wondering
what you were thinking, and now I know."
"Take care, Maura," he says.
And I say, "I guess I'll see you in May?"
He says, "Maybe. Take care of yourself."
Everyone in the living room heard my end
of the conversation, so they know. For the rest
of the day nobody bothered me in my room.
I pack my bags. At school
I won't have time to feel sorry for myself,
but here at home, I shut the door
and write it all down.

Meg
1980

When I was little and slender as a yellow reed, my uncles used to call me Twiggy, after the British model with a matchstick-like figure. But later, they started saying things like, "We can't call you Twiggy anymore," as they tried to tickle my not-so-flat middle. Now, I just try not to think about things like that. Why do hurtful comments always stick with you and never stop hurting? And why do I even care what people say about me? When people comment about my body, I think I take the words too much to heart. If people said I was stupid, I'd just know they were full of shit, but when they say I'm not thin anymore, well that cuts too close to my own worst fears about myself.

Today, we are having a family party where I'll have to see all my aunts and uncles, and I'm getting dressed and nothing is looking or feeling right. Why is my appearance always so important to me? My family is supposed to love me unconditionally.

I feel the love, all right, but I also feel the judgment too, and it makes me self-conscious. All of my uncles think it's their business to comment on my appearance as soon as we say hello. *What did you do to your hair? Did you put on a few pounds?* Or if I'm lucky, one of them will say, *You're lookin' good, sweetheart.* I'm also nervous about all the food. Too many choices and too much temptation. I know I'll have to find a place to get sick after I eat.

I think I'll wear the blue dress with the pink flowers. I'll wear my hair up. That might be fun. They are taking a big family photo since so many of us will be there. All of this makes me feel nervous pressure. Why? Larry is coming with me, so that will help.

I want to apply to Randolph-Macon for next fall. Mr. Cohen is the sponsor of *Pipeline*, and he'll write a recommendation letter for me. It's going to be harder to get the other two letters. I'm not the best student, I admit, but most of the things they want us to do in school are so worthless.

I'd be a hypocrite if I just did everything everyone told me to do. Shouldn't I be learning to think for myself? Shouldn't I be deciding how to spend my learning time? That's why I love working on the paper. I get to come up with my own story and go out there and find the truth.

You get to question authority and question people. You get to ask questions everyone else is too shy to ask. I'd even be too shy to ask, but somehow as a reporter, I give myself the permission to be brave and bold. I'll ask, *why does the star quarterback get to blow off his classes when the rest of us don't get a break? Why can't we get some decent tasting food in the cafeteria?* I was proud when my series about the cafeteria food netted us some good French fries. It feels good when people notice and thank you for helping to make a positive change in the world, so I know I want to work on the school paper wherever I end up going.

After getting into Randolph-Macon, my next goal is to get a car. I feel like I have an iron-clad case on this one. My parents sent Maura back to school this semester with the clunky green Nana car—good riddance to that evil thing! I hated driving that car. Now that they've given it to Maura, it's only fair that they'll be open to helping me get a car.

And I know exactly the one I want—it's a yellow Toyota Celica I saw at Ron's Automotive. It's not brand new so it will be more affordable, and it's totally cute. Well, it might be affordable to some people, but not really for me at this point. Still, I am determined, and I am going to put all my energy into getting this car before summer.

I don't want anybody driving me to work every day. Larry and I are going to work at the Roxbury Apartments pool this summer. It's slightly weird that last summer I worked at the Chapman Apartments pool with Mark. It's going to be hard to put Mark and last summer completely out of my mind. Mark and I had the best talks because no one ever came to that pool to swim. There were a few women who would come in to the pool, unsnap their bikini tops, and just sunbathe for a few hours. The sexy ladies got Mark all excited and we would usually end up making out in the pump room at the end of our day.

I wonder if Mark will ever become a cartoonist for *The New Yorker*. We were supposed to move to Manhattan after college and be the happy couple. He would draw his political cartoons, and I would be an investigative reporter for *The New York Times*.

I'm still in disbelief that we're not together. I have this recurring daydream where I'm driving through Charlottesville in my bright yellow car, and Mark is so glad to see me that he forgets all about Laurel, the cookie girl from Alabama.

Maura
1980

I watch the calendar and wait
for the blood and the cramps and the headache
to come on the 13th.
When they do,
I am finally able to cry—
tears of relief,
I guess, but also
tears of sorrow, because the last
chance I have
of staying connected to Joe
is washing away.

My plan for self-preservation
is to not
go home at all this summer.
I'll waitress in Oxford
and make some money and avoid
working another summer with Joe.
It would just be too awkward now.
I can't imagine it.

Mom sent a letter on legal-size paper
detailing all the ways
I've screwed up my life
with an equal number of suggestions
on how to correct the situation.
First, she writes about Joe:
He took advantage of you. You were vulnerable

and he used you. You will meet someone who will
appreciate you. Why don't you go out
and buy yourself something pretty? You don't want
to let your experiences with one person
make you negative toward them all.

I suppose I brought all this on myself
when I cried on the phone last Sunday.
I didn't mean to, but I couldn't bring
myself to say *I'm fine*
when I've been far from fine.

Mom's epistle, as she called her letter,
also talked about Meg and her concerns
that Meg's still bingeing and purging.
She can't confirm her suspicions
and she hasn't said anything because the opportunity
hasn't presented itself.
Mom thinks Larry is a positive
for Meg. They sit around the house holding hands
and making eyes at each other. A boy on the football team
died in a car crash and Mom, Meg, and Larry all went
to the memorial. Mom's letter ended by telling me
life is short.
I should try to enjoy myself.

Meg

I'm keeping things together. I'm on the go, making plans. I still have my daydreams about Mark—that I'll run into him when he's home visiting or that I'll see him at a party next year when I'm down in Virginia.

I got into R-MC! The bill is going to be high, though, because I didn't get the kind of scholarship that *Maura* got. I can't be like the *perfect* daughter, the one who, even when she does something wrong, gets sympathy instead of punishment. Poor Maura is so depressed, so let's not yell at *her* for staying out late and drinking and driving.

Just a few more months of high school. I can do it. My brain and body are always working. I keep going until I just collapse into sleep. I often wake in bed with crumpled papers and the books I was studying when I fell asleep and then just dart off to do the next day.

Sleeping is optional and some nights, I just skip it completely. I like having the run of the house when everyone else is asleep. I can eat what I want—then get rid of it. Drink what I want and get rid of that, too.

For me, it's just good to stay in a spin and keep going. That way there's never any time to have a heavy conversation with Mom or anyone else for that matter.

Larry is so sweet. He waits for me at lunch and after school. He brings me Diet 7-UP—my favorite. I like being seen with him. He's going to live at home and go to Loyola next year. He got a great scholarship. I like how serious he is, and how everyone thinks he's so brainy. He thinks eventually he might want to go to California to study film, but he says he wants to be practical right now and stay close to home. The way he dotes on me can be a little aggravating in private, but in public, I love it. Just let everybody see me being loved and spoiled. I have a secret hope that people will tell Mark and he'll get jealous and want me back.

I know all this still wanting Mark stuff is wrong, but I can't help it. I really like Larry. I can't imagine how I would have gotten through the embarrassment of being dumped by Mark without him.

My parents think Larry's some kind of golden boy, so that helps me at home with them, even though Mom and I are approaching open warfare lately. I see her wearing a hole in the blue couch and it makes me sick. She's always writing a letter to Maura, probably telling her what a pain in the ass I am. Mom's all boo-hooey about the fact that Maura doesn't want to come home this summer. No wonder Maura wants to stay away. This place is a madhouse.

All Mom wants to do is say no to everything I want. For instance, I want this car. It's still for sale, but it won't be there forever, and she will not listen. I have a job, so I'll be able to make payments, but she just won't hear me on the subject.

"Mom, it's an adorable car, good on gas. It's a Toyota. Won't you come with me to see it?"

"I don't see the point of looking at it. We have your tuition payment to make and you aren't getting enough financial aid, so a car right now is out of the question."

"But why is it impossible? I'll be making money all summer. I'll make half the cost of the car that way, and I can get some babysitting jobs, too."

"You just don't understand about cars, Meg. It isn't just buying the car, but you have the insurance, the gas, the maintenance..."

"Then why does Maura get a car? Why does she get everything, and I get nothing?" I want to know.

"Maura's driving Nana's car. We didn't have to buy it, and since it's old, the insurance payment isn't as high. You know all this, Meg."

"Yeah, but why does she automatically get it? Nana didn't leave it to her in her will or anything. Maura gets everything because she's older, and I get nothing because there's never anything left for me!"

Then Mom shrugs in that irritating way and says, "It's impossible to talk to you. I'm done. You have to have the best of everything--the most expensive school and car and clothes. We just don't have the money. If we had the money, we would loan you the money. Hell, we'd *give* you the money for the car, but we don't have it! We're sending you to your precious Randolph-Macon, and that's going to have to be enough."

That's when Dad walks in, so Mom says, "You talk to her, Hal. I'm going upstairs."

I'm seething mad and close to tears, steaming with the unfairness of life. Why couldn't I have been the first born? I would never want that ugly green car, but maybe we could trade it in for something decent.

"Dad," I say, "Mom will not even listen to me."

"What about, baby?"

"See, I found the car I need for getting to work this summer and for going to school next year. It's used, but it's been inspected. I've already test driven it, and it's perfect, but Mom won't even look at it."

"Do you have the money you need to pay for it?"

"I have enough saved for the down payment, but I

might need help to pay off the rest. I have the job at the pool, and I'll get another one. It would save you in the long run in time and money. You wouldn't have to drive me to work every day this summer," I say, making my argument.

"So, where is this perfect car?" Dad asks.

Hopeful, I tell him, "It's at the automotive place right by school. It's the yellow car parked right in front. Can we go look at it now? I'm afraid someone else might buy it if we don't act fast."

"I'll drive by this afternoon after I pick Mia up from school. She's having some kind of trouble on the bus," he says. I smother him with hugs and kisses, even though by now he's opening the paper and starting to ignore me.

"Do you think we could get it by this weekend? I could drive the whole family over to Aunt Rachel's."

"Just leave it be for now, Meg. I said I'd take a look, but I'm not making any promises."

"Thanks, Daddy. I love you, Daddy," I say to the newspaper he's holding up in front of his face.

Maura

I come home to help get ready
for Meg's graduation party.
The sun is bright; the menu is planned.
We have a big house and yard to clean
and one absentee father.
Dad's at a horticulture conference in St. Louis
until tomorrow. Mom's language is as blue
as the sky. I'm trying to stay calm and not lose it
like the rest of the females in the family
but it isn't easy. Early this morning a dump truck
unloaded an enormous pile of white stones in the
    driveway.
Dad ordered the stones months ago
and today just happens to be delivery day.
My way to cope is by putting my head down
and doing my chores. Picking lettuce and spinach
for the big salad tomorrow. Mia is with me in the garden
but she can't tell the difference between the lettuce and the
    weeds.
She has her own gathering basket and I'll just have to deal
    with
it later when I wash everything.
"I like Jay from Bible Study," Mia tells me.
"I like him, too," I agree.
"It's too hot out here. When will we be done?"
She's shoveling handfuls of dirt, bugs, and green stuff in
    her basket.
"We need a lot of lettuce for the whole crowd.
 I don't know," I tell her, carefully shaking off the extra dirt
    from my lettuce.

"'Cause I'm breakin' out
from all the itchiness. I can't stand it," Mia says.
Her arms are red and blotchy.
I can see there are more weeds and grass
than lettuce in her basket,
so I tell her to go wash off with the garden hose.
When I've filled both baskets, I head to the back porch,
where I hear Mom and Meg yelling.
"Why can't I just invite a few more friends?"
"Megan Elizabeth, the invitations are set. It's a *family*
    party.
You already invited Larry and Mindy.
That's going to have to be *it* in the friend department."
Meg continues, "But Larry and Mindy
can't even come and we're going to be outside anyway.
I just don't see why it's a big deal."
"Just drop it, Meg. I only bought enough food and drinks
for the number of people we invited."

I decide to wash the lettuce outside. I don't want to go into
the kitchen, into the middle of that. I turn up my music.

Meg

I don't know why, but I always get blamed for everything. Mom and Dad gave me this big graduation party, and it started out great. There were so many people and presents. What I want to know is, *why was it my fault that word got out and it turned into a big field party afterward?* I didn't start the rumor.

Dad came home from his trip to Missouri on the morning of the party, and Mom was a complete wreck—as usual, I might add. He was tired from his early flight, and Mom was *fit to be tied*, to use one of her crazy expressions.

Our driveway needed fixing because it had huge holes in it, so Dad had arranged for a friend to bring gravel to fill in the holes. Whoever brought the gravel was supposed to distribute it evenly across the whole driveway, but instead it was in this enormous pile that we had to spread before the guests arrived.

Mom was running around cleaning and cooking and screaming at anyone she saw. We were all trying to be helpful, but it didn't matter. If we were sweeping, she yelled that we were making dust that would get into the food. If we sat down to take a little break, she wanted to know why the hell were we sitting when there was still so much to do.

We knew we couldn't please her, so what was the point of trying? She'd be shrieking like a madwoman, and she'd stop mid-scream to say *hello* in the sweetest voice you ever heard, whenever the phone would ring.

Meanwhile, outside, Dad spread wheelbarrows full of stones. Whenever I couldn't take it inside anymore, I took Dad a glass of water. He appreciated it for a while, but then he told me to stop.

"Call that boyfriend of yours and see if he can come over and help me with this. I don't think I'm going to be able to finish it all before the party."

"He's with his dad this weekend, and he can't come over. He can't even come to the party," I told him.

"That's too bad," he agreed and got back to work.

I was upset about Larry not being able to come. It wasn't as though I didn't tell him in plenty of time; but no, he and his dad had to go fishing and it was the only time they could go. Fishing is more important than your girlfriend's graduation party? I was really pissed.

I try to sneak past Mom as I go back into the house with no luck. She gives me the job of snapping string beans, which I hate. We need them for the crab soup, so I guess it's worth it, but I hate the texture of the furry string beans and it makes me gag just to think about it.

Before I start the job, I sneak into the fridge and guzzle a beer. The cold, sloshy liquid in my stomach makes me feel sick, but I force myself to keep it down. Then I sit on the porch with the beans and start snapping off the ends.

As the alcohol starts to take effect, I feel my body relax and I don't even mind anymore that Mom's playing Neil Diamond loudly on the stereo. I even start to sing along to "Song Sung Blue," until I stop myself.

By the time guests start arriving around four o'clock, I'm feeling good. I'm wearing a yellow sundress Mom made me. I look cute, and I'm ready for the party to begin. Dad, sunburned, with a Budweiser in his hand, is dozing on a lawn chair.

From the kitchen, I hear Mom yell, "Hal, start the grill!"

My relatives arrive in droves: grandparents, aunts, uncles, and lots of cousins. Some cousins start playing guitars and singing. We make up about a hundred different verses to "May the Circle Be Unbroken" and it's fun to laugh at all the silliness. I even get my flute and play a verse. It feels good when everyone claps.

The food is amazing and everyone, including me, eats too much. I have to sneak upstairs a couple of times, but it's all good; I'm under control. As it starts to get dark, people start to leave the party.

At first, my parents don't notice that other cars are starting to park in the big field beside our house. There's a tall hedge that shields the view from the house. When I walk out to say goodbye to Aunt Rachel, I see a bunch of cars I don't recognize. There are people milling around, and my Uncle Nelson is having trouble even getting onto the road.

"Who are all these people?" Aunt Rachel asks.

"I'm not really sure," I tell her.

"Should we go over and talk to them?" she wonders.

"I don't think so," I tell her. I see one guy I recognize— Paul Dawson—our senior class president. I can't believe he's here, at my house!

"Well," Aunt Rachel says, "they better get out of the driveway, so people can get through. Maybe we should go tell your parents about this."

"Please, no!" I say. "I'll take care of it. It will just upset Mom."

"You're probably right about that. She sure is a great cook, and it was such a fun party."

"I'm so glad you could come, and thanks so much for the beautiful necklace! I love it!" I tell her.

"My pleasure, sweetheart. We're so glad you are feeling better this summer."

"Things are better. I just took the breakup with Mark too hard. I wish you could have met Larry."

"We'll meet him next time, Meg," she says, hugging me once more. Saying goodbye is a slow process at these parties.

After she drives off, Paul Dawson walks over to me and says, "We heard you were having a party, Meg. How's it going?"

I can't believe he even knows my name, but I just say coolly, "It's going pretty well."

"Do you want a beer?" he asks me.

"Well, sure. Okay," I say.

We walk over to his blue Mustang and he opens the door. "Hand me a beer," he says to someone I can't see.

"You need another one already?" his girlfriend Alyssa says.

"It's not your business, but I'm giving one to Meg—this is her house."

"Can I use your bathroom?" Alyssa leans out and asks me.

"Sure, okay," I say and then I wonder how I'm going to get her in and out of my house without my parents seeing.

I chug the beer and hand the can back to Paul.

"Impressive," he says.

I walk back up the drive with Alyssa, who I don't really know.

There's an awkward moment when I pass Maura without saying anything. No luck keeping this from Mom and Dad now, I think. Maura is like a third parent instead of a sister.

I don't see Mom or Dad, though, and I end up spending lots of time out in the field with Paul and Alyssa and a bunch of other people, too.

I smuggle some beer out of our kitchen, and at some point, I make out with a guy named Dan Green. I remember drinking more beers and throwing up in the cornstalks.

There's also this vague memory of red and blue police lights and someone—was it Maura? —helping me up the steps to my bedroom.

I sleep late the next day and wake up to cold silence in the house. I go out into the field with a black trash bag and start picking up beer cans and glass bottles and cigarette butts.

Dad helps me, and he tries to yell at me, but he takes pity. I can barely stand, and my skin has a green color and the circles under my eyes make it look like I've been punched.

"Who invited all these people here?" he asks.

"Not me," I tell him, which is true. "I didn't know half of them."

"Look, Meg. I was able to convince the officers last night that we weren't providing alcohol to minors because technically most of those kids were parked off our property, and I was the one who called the police, anyway. But they made thirteen arrests, and you're lucky you weren't one of them. If Maura hadn't dragged you out of that mess, I don't know what would have happened."

"Dad, I'm sorry. Really. I didn't know."

"Well, you damn right better start knowing. Your mother is just beside herself. After all she did to give you a nice party. You'd best steer clear of her today. And for the rest of the summer, young lady, you need to be on your best behavior, because we're not sending you off to school if you can't show us you're going to use the good sense God gave you. Do you understand me?"

Maura

Sitting in a sterile room
counting change on an ugly
synthetic bedspread
is not how I pictured my summer.

I give most of my earnings
from waitressing
to Miss Jean Pickens,
a stout widow who
is renting me a room in her brick rancher.

I don't feel comfortable here
even though the house is clean and quiet
and it sits near the water.
My every move seems so loud.
I don't want to disturb Miss Jean.
My food in the refrigerator has its own shelf.

It doesn't help that I've discovered
I'm the world's worst waitress.
Mom says to give it time,
but I think I'm hopeless. I go
into the Pier Street Marina
with an open mind, but three tables
in I've already made so
many blunders, I'm ready to quit.
People want too many things—all at the same time.
The highchair is dirty. What am I supposed to do
about that? I spill a glass of water.
Coffee is at one

side of the restaurant and soda is at the other.
If I get coffee first, it will be cold when I serve it.
I go to pick up an order. Two people order the same meal—
one looks delicious, the other looks dry and skimpy.
Who wants to hear that I've noticed this? No one.
Just get out of here and serve it!
I'm thinking that one table is going
to ask for the check, but they decide they want pie
and ice cream
and coffee!
The pie needs heating.
I dig my dirty hands
into the vanilla ice cream.
When I get to the coffee station, I see
the empty pot. Even the payment part is frustrating.
I'm too slow with every single part of this job.

I do find some comfort
in counting my tips.

I guess I should be glad
I didn't get fired.
I give my notice in July
and two weeks later I drive home
to Boring, Maryland in Nana's car.
I'm happy to leave. The trip
is glorious. I ride in the clouds.

Before long I turn into our drive
and see the red barn. Mom's gardens
are beautiful. The black-eyed Susans
and red impatiens are in full bloom. Mom

is kneeling in the dirt. She looks up
to say, "Welcome home!"

Meg

Because Maura's home, our parents decide we're going to take a little family vacation. I can't help but resent that *Maura* is the reason we get to celebrate. Still, I want to go on the trip, and I manage to get a sub, so Larry won't have to work alone for three days.

Despite everything, I'm glad to see Maura. With the college bills due, we can't do anything big, but Dad wants to go clamming and Mom says, "It won't be summer if I can't hear the ocean." We take off and once we get Mom over the bay bridge, we can feel freedom, like a current, carry us to the shore. Our place is on the bay side, probably a dump.

Driving down here, Dad can't shut up about clams. "The most delicious clams I ever ate, I found in a little shack at a place called Galilee Beach in Rhode Island. I think I was about ten years old and I was there with..." Dad does love to drone on and on about his seafood.

Maura and I roll eyes at each other in the back seat. It feels strange to all be together again in the Oldsmobile station wagon. Mia sits in between us, randomly whacking us with her pillow as she tries to nap. It's a nuisance, but having her awake would be even more annoying, so we tolerate it.

"We need to find a guy with a boat to take us out, about two hours before low tide," Dad continues. "Did everyone bring old tennis shoes?" he asks.

"Yes, Hal," Mom says in her exasperated tone, "Let Mia sleep."

"There are some people who like to find the clams with their feet," Dad continues, obliviously, "but I think we'll do better with shoes and a rake."

Mom sighs loudly.

If I knew sign language, I'd tell Maura, *thank you for keeping me from getting arrested in June.* I'd ask her *how does it feel to be away from home on your own?* Since I can't ask, I just rest my head against the window and doze.

I awaken, startled, as we cross the Route 50 Bridge. I feel my stomach rumble. I drank a Bloody Mary before we left this morning and ate four chewable vitamins. I just mix the Old Bay and V8 in the kitchen and then take it upstairs and add the vodka. Nobody's the wiser.

I think maybe I had a bad dream or something. I have a vague feeling that I was rolling in my yellow car. There's broken glass and twisted metal, but in the dream, I get out and walk away. I'm glad it's just a dream, because I love my car.

I shake off the weird feelings and think *we're almost at the beach!*

Dad says, "Let's go right to the beach, and we'll find our place later." No arguments—we all just want to see the water. We find a place to park. Maura gives Mia a little nudge.

I have my blue and green suit on, and I start walking toward the ocean, but Mom calls me back for sunscreen.

"Mom, I'm in the sun every freaking day. I'm not going to burn," I tell her.

"Watch your mouth," she says, as she smooths the cool, white lotion on my shoulders.

"What? What did I say?" I ask.

"Here," Mom says, "Let me get your back. The sun is different down here."

Maura

I share a bed with Meg
in this creepy little beach house
where we're staying.
We got roasted like lobsters
on the beach and bitten by mites
when we were clamming
so I'm not comfortable enough to sleep.

Meg must be having a bad dream.
She keeps calling out,
but I can't understand what she's saying.

Captain Jim found us a good spot
to dig near the bird sanctuary island.
Mia is in a tizzy, bouncing around
in her little white cap.
I like to hear the sound
the rake makes against the clam shells.
Mom's hat keeps blowing off.
Her laughter is a good sound, too.
I find at least a dozen clams.
Each one fills my hand.
Captain Jim keeps saying, "I'm watching the tide!"
The water gets deeper and we get called
back to the boat. We haul the rakes
and our bags filled with clams.
I look over at Meg and she's splattered with mud.
It's funny to see her
so undone—without the makeup and perfect hair,
she looks relaxed and completely happy.

"Keep the clams in saltwater
so they can purge all the sand and mud.
You'll be able to see all the sand
at the bottom of the bucket
in just a few hours," Dad tells us.
I catch Meg's eye and we bubble with laughter
at this Dad of ours and his random clam knowledge.
We can't stop giggling when he tells us
again how much he loves the soft-bellied steamers.

Later, the small cherrystones
get eaten raw. Dad shows us how
to open the shells and even Mia tries them.
The rest are cooked in wine and butter
and served over linguine. We stay outside
until the bugs get bad.
Then we take a drive to the beach.
Mom and Dad go off together
holding hands.
Meg and I exchange another look over that.
"Clams bring out the best in Dad," Meg says.
"Totally," I agree. Mia is talking with a guy
who's flying a kite. He lets her hold it,
and she yells, "Wheeeeee!"
"We all needed this," says Meg.
"Things got a little intense in June."
"Was there any fallout from the field party?
I've been afraid to bring it up," I say.
"A bunch of people got arrested. I think I'm grounded
till college, but they did pay the deposit, so I guess
they'll let me go," Meg says.
"Are you doing okay? I don't think I've seen anyone

as drunk as you were that night," I say.

"Yeah, I did get messed up. I don't remember much. Dad said
you saved me from the slammer. Thanks for that," Meg says.

"Anything for my little sister," I say.

"Where's the camera?" Meg says. "I want to remember this day."

Meg

The whole month of August, I'm working at the pool, getting stuff together for college, teaching swim lessons, and barely sleeping. I have bad dreams when I do sleep. I see a yellow dragon. It's loud and repulsive. It's always coming towards me, but I wake up before it gets me.

I start seeing things when I'm awake, too, weird things when I'm looking out my bedroom window. I see "bad guys" in the trees in broad daylight. I start to worry about myself a little, but then I calm myself down and tell myself I must be stressed about going away to school.

On the outside, I'm Meg, the lifeguard, heading to college and a bright future, but nobody sees what's inside. I want it all—the food, the fun, the flat belly. If I make a mistake, there's always a way to fix it.

The pool where Larry and I are lifeguards is busier than the one where Mark and I worked. There are so damn many kids pestering us from opening to closing. I feel like Larry and I are the babysitters for the neighborhood. A whole posse of squirmy kids are waiting at the gate when we arrive to open at 10 a.m. They follow us around all day and never stop talking to us or fighting among themselves. The noise drives me crazy, but Larry is more patient.

I make sure nobody—especially Larry or Mindy—sees me feeling sad. I don't want anyone to know I still miss Mark and can't get him out of my head.

Mia is chirping about one boy or another. Bible study turns out to be a boyfriend goldmine for her. First Tad, then Roger, then George. She has boys calling all the time. Sometimes she comes to the pool with me to work on her tan. Her constant chitchat drives me nuts. I envy her, though, because she never seems to get hurt if one boy stops liking her. She just eagerly goes on to the next boy without a care in the world.

I, on the other hand, feel like I'm stuck in quicksand. No matter how sweet Larry is—and he is so sweet—I just can't stop thinking about Mark.

As college orientation approaches, I get more excited and nervous. One Saturday, Mom surprises me by taking me to Towson, my favorite place to shop. We find enough basement bargains to keep her happy, and I love it all. Blazers and blouses and sweaters, oh my! We can barely carry everything in one trip. We try on so many shoes, and then we go to lunch—crab bisque and spinach salad. Best of all, we don't fight all day.

There are the quick kind of goodbyes—see ya soon! And then there are the longer ones, like the goodbye that was hard to say when Mom and Dad dropped me off at Randolph-Macon.

Mom is almost sobbing. Dad is choking up, but I'm holding it together. I hug them tight, tell them I'll miss them, then run off to start my new life.

I meet lots of friends because of Randy and Diane. I knew them in high school, and we've kept in touch. Randy's like a teddy bear big brother to me. He takes me to parties, laughs at my jokes, and takes me home when I get sloshed.

People are just friendlier here than they are at home. I make friends with these girls I just can't believe. They wear ribbons in their hair and do exotic things like play lacrosse and show horses.

My roommate Vivian is one of these girls. She has a boyfriend at VMI, and she goes to see him every weekend.

That works out well for Larry and me. Larry's living at home, so he's ready for lots of road trips to Ashland, unless he's got a big project or something.

When Larry comes down, we always go out. He meets my friends and puts up a good front, but I don't think he has too much fun. I'm having the time of my life. It's like one continuous party. The silliest things strike me as funny, and I can't stop laughing.

Still, Larry sticks by me. Some mornings I wake up not sure about what happened the night before. He doesn't seem to mind if I let loose and have a good time.

What I'm not doing is studying. I mean, I go to some of my classes, but I'm missing deadlines and failing some tests.

When I have a paper to write, I stay up all night and write it. When I hand it in, I think it's the greatest thing I've ever written, but when I get it back, I'm usually embarrassed by how bad it is, if I can even force myself to reread it.

I keep making promises to myself that I'll improve and behave myself and do my best, but then I keep messing up and doing the exact opposite of what I want to do.

There are dates that just stop the clock. For me, that day is October 17th. It starts as the best of days. It's a Saturday, perfect in every discernible way: blue sky, crisp breeze, and bright sun. I'm heading across the quad to the store with crimson and gold leaves flashing in the sun.

Larry's coming down tonight, and I want to make it a special night for just the two of us. I've pushed the limits of his patience lately, and I want to make it up to him.

I'm getting wine and cheese and chocolate-covered

strawberries. I'm cleaning the room of one hundred years of dust and sweat, and I'm getting myself all spiffed up. All of this takes great effort, but it's a labor of love.

Love of Larry? I'm not sure. Love of romance? Maybe. Love of being in control of my own destiny? Absolutely.

As I'm walking in Ashland, I remember that Mom and Dad and Mia are at the beach this weekend. Mom's there for the Maryland State Teachers Convention with a bunch of her friends from the elementary school where she works as an aide with the preschoolers. I think back to our trip to Ocean City in July—was it only three months ago?— and I hope they are having fun.

By the time Larry arrives at 3 p.m., I'm ready. There are just days when you know you look fantastic. Most days, I can get frantic about my hair, but today it falls perfectly to my shoulders. I put on a little black dress I found at a consignment shop. I feel like Jackie O, like American royalty.

Larry walks in the room. He looks nice, but not quite good enough for me on this particular day. He's wearing khakis and a striped polo. I can't exactly make him change his clothes, can I?

We go to Ferdinand's for dinner. I wish we could sit in the bar. I feel every eye looking at me. Things are going perfectly.

As we drive back to campus, I think to myself, "Today is as good as life gets." Here I am looking great with this handsome guy who adores me, and we're going back to my immaculate and soon to be candlelit dorm room.

I'm excited about my surprises. I want Larry to have a piece of cheese or a strawberry, but he's too full from dinner. I want him to turn around and not look until I say so. He smiles a forgiving smile when he turns around and sees me in a pale green skimpy nightgown.

We probably have three hours of bliss, three hours of loving and being loved, before Cassie Engelmann, my RA, starts banging on my door. It takes a while before I realize the knocking isn't going to stop unless I do something.

I get up and put my bathrobe on. I let a small crack of light into the room.

"Meg, you're here," Cassie says, breathless.

"Obviously," I say.

"Meg, I got a phone call. Can I come in and talk to you?"

"Cassie, what is it? I was asleep," I say.

"Oh, Meg," she says and starts to cry.

Maura

And suddenly, I'm Bambi
paralyzed in the woods
without my mother.

I have moments in the morning
before I'm fully awake
when I feel the promise of a new day
and then I remember:
Mom is gone.

They were coming home from dinner
on Ocean Boulevard, when a sixteen-year-old driver
slammed into the car where Mom and Dad
were passengers. Dad is expected to survive.

Mia was riding in a car behind
with some of Mom's friends,
so she wasn't in the accident.

At eighteen, you shouldn't have to pick
out your mother's burial clothes,
but that's what Meg is doing today.
It makes no sense.

I'm still in Salisbury with Dad. The accident
that killed my mother is keeping my dad in the hospital
with too many broken bones to count.

Some nuns have opened a room for me
in a nearby convent. I walk back and forth each day

and I'm grateful for their kindness and the numb way
I feel in such alien surroundings.

Meg is home alone with Mia. Dear God,
I can't imagine it. I can't imagine
a world without my mother in it.

What happens if Dad isn't well enough
to travel home for Mom's funeral on Saturday?
He needs to be there. We need him to be there.

"I picked her blue dress," says Meg
on the phone. "I'm sorry,
you have to do that," I say.
"I want to do something," she says,
"I feel so helpless. How is Dad doing?"
She wants to know. "He's loopy," I say,
"They have him on something."
"What are we going to do?" she wonders.
I tell her, "I have no idea."

.

Meg

Important jobs fall to me. There is no one else who can do them. I have to talk to people on the phone—priests, funeral directors, Catholic people I don't know. My uncle tells me what to do, and I don't argue with him.

Shouldn't we wait till Dad's out of the hospital? Why do we have to rush? They tell me to take an outfit to Eline's Funeral Home. I open her closet, and she is there. L'Air Du Temps was her fragrance. The metal hangers scrape—she hated all these dresses! I pick something blue. It's linen and lined with a silky white fabric. I don't remember seeing her in this dress, but it's pretty. I don't want to think about her wearing this for all eternity. I find a scarf; that's better. It's chartreuse green, sheer and sparkly, the color of Ireland.

I deal with Mia's hyper-hysterical phase—the loud sobbing, not quite sincere. I'm glad she can't feel this death the way I feel it.

I arrange all the food we will serve. There is so much food. To keep from gagging, I think of it like furniture or boxes to be moved. I try not to lean over. I keep myself in a state of low buzz—not sober, not drunk. Aunt Rachel calls me stoic.

My grandmother hugs me so hard I think my bones will snap. I hold onto Larry's arm at the wake. Behind dark glasses, clutching his arm, sipping vodka, I make it through the first five days.

Maura tells me that Mark came to the funeral. "Who cares?" I say.

I go back to Randolph-Macon to get my stuff. I have to withdraw. I have no interest in school. My friends surround me in a circle. They are a consolation. But I must go home. My daddy needs me.

Larry helps me pack up the boxes and load them into our two cars. I look at him differently now, in this new world of loss. He is a quiet shepherd, and he leads me back home.

Maura

I go back to school after two weeks.
If I don't go back now, I never will.
Leave my dad in a hospital bed in our living room,
leave my two younger sisters alone,
and run away.

Nobody blames me. Nobody
begs me to stay. Meg *wants*
to stay, she says. She'll try again at Towson,
maybe next fall. Studying is the last thing
she wants to do right now. I feel horrible
that she is taking on the burden
of Dad, of Mia. I feel horrible
that she is giving up Randolph-Macon,
her journalism dreams. But that doesn't stop me.
I drive off in the ugly green car
with my half-read copy of *Moby Dick*
thrown in the back seat.

Meg
1981

By the spring after Mom's death, I'm the only one who doesn't have prescribed painkillers, Prozac, or a bereavement support group. It's hilarious, really. They call me the strong one.

Dad's on so many meds, all he can do is make jokes. He laughs at his own jokes until his cracked ribs make him stop. His favorite joke has something to do with how Mom always got mad when he left the cap off the toothpaste. I guess laughter is his way of coping, but it drives Maura crazy. When he won't stop, she storms off. Not that she's here that much anyway.

Mia performs a one-woman play called *Emotional Meltdown* for anyone brave enough to visit. If someone agrees to sit with Dad, then I get a little break. That's when I call Larry and say, "Come get me out of this nuthouse!"

Larry always comes through like a champ. He holds my hand, lacing his long fingers with mine. He listens patiently as I talk about how I want to transfer to Towson and how I want to take more classes so that the two of us can graduate together as planned. He sympathizes when I complain about Mia. He nods when I ask if he thinks I look cute in this pink outfit. He doesn't protest—too much—when I say no to sex. I want to hold his hand, but for some reason, now I can barely stand to be kissed.

We drive all the way down to Bengies Drive-In for a date night when it opens for the season. We're seeing *The Empire Strikes Back*. I never saw the first *Star Wars* movie, but Larry says I'll catch on. He's really into it.

We wait in a long line to get in and a longer line for

popcorn, but the popcorn's good, and it's fun to be here. We're in his mother's Buick with the bench seat in the front so we can cuddle. The music starts playing, and I scooch closer. There's a lot of yellow text on the screen. I can't read it all. Luke Skywalker. Darth Vader. Blah, blah, blah.

I kiss his ear and whisper, "I think we should get married."

"What?" he says, "Watch the movie. This is an important part." He's already seen the movie. I could care less about the movie.

I repeat, "I think we should get married." He shakes his head at me and laughs. He focuses on the screen. Luke has just been attacked by the Abominable Snowmonster or something.

When he ignores me, I say, "Just forget it then," and I pout.

"Don't get mad, baby. I just want to see this," he says crunching on popcorn.

"This is so ridiculous," I shrug, referring to the movie.

"Meg, we came all the way down here to see this. It's great. Just watch the movie."

"I didn't come here to see *Star Wars*; I came to be with you," I say this with my hand under his shirt, my head on his shoulder. He doesn't respond to my touch, so I move away from him, all the way to the door.

The movie continues, but within minutes, I'm asleep.

Maura

I have my first Thanksgiving,
my first Christmas,
and my only 21st birthday,
all without my mother.
In some ways, I feel closer to her than ever.
I never stop thinking about her.
If something good happens,
she's the first person I want to tell.
I have moments when I think
I can't wait to tell her about...
and then I remember.
I have her letters though.
When I need her,
I open the zippered canvas pouch
and read and reread the letters.
I cry on them,
study them for clues.
They help me to keep
hearing her voice. I don't want to forget
her voice and her laugh.

I write about her for the poetry workshop
and even though I think
there are things I should change in my poem,
nobody makes any suggestions.

In Mother's Garden

I follow blue print written on a palm
now buried like a tottering heart
under a quilt of baby's breath.
Trace the lines of purple, basil seeds;
Coarse lifelines of sage and thyme.

First to clear the patch of onion grass.
Yank stubborn roots. Shake clumps of brown.
My gloves will be dark; geranium my perfume.
Mimicking your work, I bring tiny sticks
to mark rows, dig with a plastic shovel,
plant, water, press to make smooth.

Some tea later or perhaps a bath
of steamy mint. Potpourri in a jar
by the window. A petal pillow
in a drawer with clothes we would wear
if lavender could cloud the hurt
of afternoon; if brown hands
could gather earth and make it breathe.

Meg

I sell hats, scarves, and gloves at Macy's, and they like my work. Sometimes they use the word *capable* in my reviews. I see things all the time that I want to buy for myself or for my sisters, but even with the employee discount, it adds up. My classes at Towson are going well, which means I'm too busy to think about how they are really going. I do like them, though. They are practical and interesting, and I'm keeping up with the work. I think Communications will end up being my major.

I have a mounting pile of parking tickets. I'm always in a rush, so I don't have the luxury of being able to park in the perfect place every time. I do my best.

Basically, I want to be out of school, so I can get on with my life. Larry is still in the picture. I got him to agree that we could *talk* about getting married. He tries to be the practical one.

He says, "I'm not saying I don't *ever* want to get married. I'm just saying both of us are still in school right now. It doesn't make any sense, Meg."

"Why does everything need to make sense?" I counter.

"There's a lot going on. You've been though a lot this year. We don't need to rush. I'm not going anywhere," he says.

Like a baby, I whimper, "I just need to know that eventually, we are going to get married. I need this."

"Okay, Meg, I promise. Just not right now. We've got to be smart about this," he says.

I smile into his collar and breathe in the clean smell of his skin.

Maura

Meg tells everyone that she and Larry are engaged
as the anniversary of Mom's death approaches.
In my mind, I hear Mom's voice:
Jesus H. Christ, what in the hell
is that girl thinking? What are they going
to do for money? Are they going to live
in a tent under the Jones Falls Expressway? Neither of
*   them*
must have a lick of sense! I fight the urge
to join the chorus of dissent; nobody
besides Meg
thinks this is a good idea.

I want to support Meg. I'm grateful she is looking
out for Dad and Mia. She seems stronger to me—
like she's taking care of herself, too. She sounds rational
and grown-up when she talks about paying our property
    taxes
and other things about our house I've never thought about
    before.
She wants Mia on birth control, even though Dad says
that will just put ideas in Mia's head. I keep thinking:
she's a lot like Mom. She's taking care of all of us.

She's still drinking though. I see a bottle of vodka lying
on her bed one day. When I mention it, she says,
"I'm making a punch for my friend Daisy's party.
It has cranberry juice, lemonade, and 7-UP. You'll love
    Daisy;
she's so much fun!" And then Meg's gone again

in a blur of fancy new clothes from Macy's
and I'm left standing there wondering
if I'm worrying about nothing. She seems fine.

Dad is no help figuring anything out. He is more
and more passive. The hospital bed is gone,
but he takes the stairs slowly. He moves
like an invalid, but he's back to work.
The house and the yard are looking better.
He's got a crew digging a pond in the backyard.
He stands out there and leans against the shovel.
He offers Mom's rings to Meg. He may not
be all for the wedding, but he's not going
to stand in their way.

Meg and Larry are on the porch
when I hear this conversation from the kitchen:
"I thought we agreed this wedding stuff
was for *after we graduate.* Why
is everyone congratulating me?"
"Don't get mad. I just told Mindy what you said,
you know, about our future, and I guess she
told her mom, so Dad found out, but guess what he said?"
"What did he say?"
"He said I could have Mom's wedding and engagement
    rings.
Isn't that sweet? So, you wouldn't have to buy
me a ring and that will save us money."
"Look, Meg. *When* we get engaged, I will *want* to buy you
a ring and surprise you with it."
Larry sounds agitated, which is unusual for him.
"Let's talk about it later,"

Meg goes on,
"I think I do want to wear my mom's rings. This is the
    most
important thing Dad has ever given me."
I hear Larry sigh.

Meg

I'm busy planning for Christmas. I want it to be nice for everyone. I bought a ragg wool sweater for Maura and a pocketbook for Mia because I found an old spiral notebook where Mom had written that she wanted to get those gifts for them.

I feel a little hurt that I wasn't on the list, but I guess Dad wasn't either. He looks frail to me, so I do things around the house to cheer him up.

I get the tree with Larry's help—it's a Frazier fir, and Mia helps me decorate. It hurts to look at Mom's favorite ornaments.

I pre-order a turkey. Maura is coming home in two days.

I'm out shopping after my shift, and I just black out. Not sure how, but I end up at the emergency room. I know I went to work as usual, and I remember being in the aisle at Safeway, but after that, it's blank. I try, but I can't remember anything.

They take blood and decide to admit me. I hear someone say anemia, but I don't ask any questions. They ask *me* a lot of questions, but I'm careful not to give too many details.

Maura hovers over me as I open my eyes. I'm not sure where I am, but it's a big room. I feel paranoid and wonder what people are saying about me.

"Hey, Meg," Maura says.

"Hey yourself," I say.

"Man, you gave us a scare."

"What happened? I can't remember anything."

"Well, when I got home yesterday, no one was there.

And I finally get this weird call from Dad. He had gotten a call to come to Hopkins right away. I guess they got numbers from something in your purse."

"Shit. Where's my stuff now?"

"They gave it to Dad, and he finally just went home to rest," Maura says.

"What day is it anyway?" I can feel my heart accelerating.

"It's Thursday, December 19th. It looks like you might have to spend your birthday in here."

"Are you kidding?" I say.

"No, I'm not. The doctors are concerned. They had trouble finding a good vein for the bloodwork and IV. They say you have anemia and jaundice—that you show signs of chronic malnutrition. This is serious stuff, Meg."

"Well, I feel fine now. Where's Larry? Does he know?"

"He was here for a while. They were asking us questions because they couldn't ask you."

"Just great," I snap. "What did you tell them?"

"I didn't say much, Meg. I didn't know what to say, but we're all worried about you."

"There's nothing to worry about. What did Dad say?" I grill her.

"I don't know, Meg. Just calm down, okay?"

I start to panic. What do they know? I look down at my arms and see big purple and yellow bruises. I hate getting blood drawn, getting shots. Just the thought makes me sick. I see that I'm hooked up to a couple of IV bags. I feel like bugs are crawling all over me, and I want to rip out the IV. I need to get out of here!

This is the moment when Mia decides to speak up. She's sitting in a big reclining chair. "This is your pee,

Meg," Mia says, pointing to something at the end of the bed.

"Shut up!" I yell. "Get her the hell out of here," I say to Maura.

"It's really dark for pee," Mia continues. "It looks brown."

"Maura, I swear, if you don't get her out of here right now..." I threaten.

"Relax, Meg, we're going," Maura says. "Come on, Mia. I'll buy you a Coke."

"What did I say?" Mia says too loudly as they leave the room.

Seconds pass. I want to scream or cry. "That was classy," I hear someone say. I nearly jump out of my skin with surprise. I see a curtain and realize I must have a roommate. A female roommate. A sarcastic female roommate.

"Excuse me?" I say in my *don't mess with me* voice.

"A real class performance there," says the voice behind the curtain.

I'm in no mood. "As if it's your business," I say, surprised at my own rudeness.

"I think it is my business if it wakes me up. It's hard to get any real sleep in here," she says.

Okay, so now I feel lousy. "Sorry," I say. "I'll be quiet now. I didn't know anyone was there."

"That's because I'm so good at making myself disappear," she says.

We stop talking then. I need to think. What am I going to do? I don't want to spend my birthday in the hospital. How am I going to get out of this place?

Maura

I toy with prayer a little.
Find myself waiting by Mom's grave,
just waiting there. There's a neighbor
across the street who has cancer.
I see him lose his hair, have trouble walking
down the front steps, but I keep seeing him.
He is still in the fight.
I say to myself
the prayers are working.

I say prayers for Meg: for her body,
mind, and spirit. For God's will to be done.
I pray she'll get the help she needs.
I visit her at Hopkins, and except
for the bruises, she looks fine. She wants to leave
but she needs to stay and get better. I hope
I won't say anything
that will upset her, alienate her. Our relationship
feels fragile, like a robin's egg.

I bring her a birthday present—a set
of hairbrushes with wooden handles. I think
I'll brush her hair, if she lets me. Mom used to
do that, and one of the brushes is supposed to detangle.
I bring the things she's asked for: mascara, deodorant,
whitening toothpaste, chewable vitamins. I don't
bring Mia with me this time.

Meg laughs about having to eat mystery meat
and boiled potatoes. She wants a crab cake.

Turns out, she spends her birthday
and Christmas in the hospital. Mia,
Dad, and I spend a dismal Christmas Day
at home eating the turkey Meg ordered for us
and opening a few presents.
"Is Meg going to be okay?" Mia asks.
"Sure, Squirt," Dad says. "Don't worry about her.
She's just getting her strength up."

We pack up some things for Meg
and head down to Hopkins for visiting hours.
It's quiet there, and Meg isn't in her room.
We find her down the hallway
with her roommate, Ruth Carson,
a columnist for *The Sun*.
She's famous and Meg is awestruck
they are sharing a room. They laugh
about something as we approach. Both
have rolling IV poles with them, but Ruth
is in a wheelchair and she looks like she's in bad shape.
Her frosted hair is still pretty, but she's swollen all over
and her skin has a strange, greenish tone.
"Merry Christmas!" Mia shouts.
"The devoted family arrives," says Ms. Carson.
"Here, I'll take you back to the room," Meg tells her.
"No, no. I'll just rest here a while.
Why don't you all go down to the lounge?"
"Sounds good," says Dad.
"I'll be back in a while," Meg says before leaving with us.

"So, how's it going?" Dad asks

once we are drinking sodas in the lounge.

"Okay, I guess. I've only seen a doctor one time, and he didn't

have much to say. I don't know why they're keeping me, or

when they're going to let me out. I'm worried about Ruth, though.

She's been here for weeks, and they keep taking her

downstairs to drain fluids from her abdomen."

"Gross," says Mia.

"The first night they brought her in, they thought she was going to die."

"What's wrong with her?" I ask.

"I'm not sure, exactly," says Meg.

"It might be something to do with her liver.

I'm glad she's here, though.

It's scary at night. This is the Psych floor

and there are some wild sounds in the dark."

"What kinds of sounds?" I want to know.

"Well, last night, it sounded like someone

was throwing furniture. There was crashing

and yelling and a lot of running up and down the halls.

I think they locked some guy in a room

until the security guards came."

"That doesn't sound very safe," says Dad.

"Just see if you can get me out of here soon.

Okay, Dad?"

"I'll do what I can," says Dad.

Meg

The woman behind the curtain in my hospital room turns out to be Ruth Carson, my favorite writer. I remember her from the eating disorders group at Immanuel Hospital, but she doesn't recognize me. Now, here we are together at a different hospital. Weird.

Not much is going on at Hopkins over the holidays, so we get to know each other. She's kind of bossy. I'm more mobile than she is, and she wants me to move her pillow, get her a blanket, or turn the lights off and on.

Sometimes she wants me to read to her, but it's not like we have the best reading material. I read magazine articles aloud, and we make fun of them.

We end up discussing anorexia and bulimia as journalists. I'll be her research assistant, and we plan a series of articles.

We brainstorm a list of people to interview, people to blame. We ponder some big questions: *Is our obsession with thinness a cultural obsession? Why are some people able to ignore the pressure to look a certain way and others so susceptible to it? Is addiction to food like other addictions?*

Talking to her like this is liberating. We can define the problem and conquer it. We talk about what we'll do when we get out of here. We'll drink our vitamin drinks. Our series will win a Pulitzer.

"How old are you, Meg?" Ruth asks.

"Eighteen; no, I just turned nineteen," I say.

"I was living large at nineteen, Meg. Not a care in the world. I thought I was indestructible. But you can see, I was wrong about that. I'm thirty-five, and they tell me my liver is barely functioning. I might not get a chance to fix all this. You be careful, you hear?"

Ruth and I toast the New Year, 1982, with ginger ale; we're practically alone on the hall.

Larry, Dad, Maura, and Mia left a little while ago, left me to deal with the long night. Where are Ruth's visitors, I wonder? She has lots of cards and a chic little Rosemary Christmas tree with white lights, but no visitors. I'm curious, but don't ask.

"I want to go dancing," I tell her.

"You have time for that," she says.

"We're both getting better," I say.

"Tell me," she says. "Tell me the truth about why you are here."

"I just had a little setback. My mom died in a car crash two years ago, and I'm having trouble keeping things under control. I'll be okay, though. I'm fine, really.

"I wish I could promise you that I'll help you when you get out of here," she says. "I don't think this is the kind of illness you can beat all by yourself. I've tried to do that, and it hasn't turned out too well."

Two days later, there are doctors everywhere, and they set my discharge date. I want to tell Ruth, but she's not in the room. She doesn't come back either. I notice that a nurse is taking the cards from her bedside table, putting Ruth's hairbrush in a plastic bag. I want them to leave her things alone. What's going on?

The nurses won't talk to me or answer my questions about Ruth, so I pitch a fit, and finally they send a chaplain to tell me that Ruth has bleeding in her brain and it's just a matter of time. I ask if I can see her, and the answer's no.

Only family members are allowed in the ICU.

I'm completely numb. I sit in an office that feels like an Arctic wind tunnel. It's a bleak January day. Dad's there with me. It seems like he's in a fog. My lips are turning blue. Three people enter the room. The main doctor is there. I saw him once, and I don't know his name. Sophia, the gorgeous nutritionist, is there. I remember her brilliant advice was that I start to eat four meals a day. I look at her flawless skin and wonder how much she weighs.

The psychiatrist, Dr. Watson, drones on and on. *Could someone please get me a blanket?* I think this, but don't say it aloud. Commitment to health *blah blah blah* all the help you need *blah blah blah*. I sign their papers. I would have done anything to get out of that room. Anything.

Someone wheels me out of the front door of the hospital, and then I get into Dad's Oldsmobile.

"That was strange," is Dad's first comment.

"Welcome to my world," I reply.

"How are you feeling? Do you want some lunch?" he asks.

"A little seafood?" I suggest.

"I know just the place."

We go to a little dive bar by the water, and I eat enough for two people. The food has a narcotic effect. The little fried clams take the pain away for a few minutes. We wash them down with a couple of beers. I'm happy to have my life back.

Maura

Someone should have told me:
You are entering
the summer of bridesmaid hell.

I get fitted for and must wear
in public
three of the most hideous dresses
you could imagine. Dresses of this sort
are best worn by girls
who would look good
in a burlap sack. I am not
one of those girls.

Meg, hoping for her own
wedding soon, wants to go with me
to look at all these dresses.
We travel the Delmarva Peninsula
pondering the sight of my reflection
in a cloud of misty green toilet paper-
like substance. "I won't make you wear
something like that in my wedding," Meg says,
her head tilting sideways to take in the sight.
"Small consolation," I say, as I try
to swirl and get a view that doesn't
make me look like I belong on the cover
of a magazine called *Bridesmaid Nightmares*.

Moving means I get stuck with pins.
The dress is crooked in the front
or maybe I am. Something doesn't look

right. There is no way you should do this
to someone you call a friend. These dresses
are itchy, poorly made, designed to last
about five hours tops.

Nearing the end of one of the receptions
of that summer, a silky red one I was wearing
fell apart. The elastic gave way
on one shoulder and I had to hold the whole
monstrosity up with two hands before someone
found a safety pin in her purse.

I understand that somewhere in the universe
there might be a dress that looks good on me
but this summer I'm disgusted with my body.
The dress fitters warn, "You'd better not gain any
weight before the wedding!" There is no forgiveness
in these dresses; either the zipper goes up or it doesn't.

I'm jealous of the way
Meg looks in a smaller version
of this pink dress I'm wearing.
She's tiny and adorable
and tries it on just for fun.
She smiles and spins
and tries on three more.
I don't think she means
to rub salt in my wounds.

At lunch, she tells me she's doing well.
She's developing healthy patterns, she says,
but she doesn't say what that means.

I have a salad
and she has a Rueben sandwich with fries.
I'm drinking water, and she wants me to order her
a Margarita. Just making conversation, I say,
"Have you stayed in touch with Ruth Carson?"
"Don't want to talk about it," she says,
her mouth full of food. "Okay," I say,
"it just seems like you two were getting close."
"Pass me the salt, would you?"
"How's Larry doing?" I try instead.
"He's a little too into movies, if you ask me."
"What kind of movies?" I ask.
"Oh, I don't know," she says,
"Can we talk about something else?"

Meg

I get the house in tiptop shape. I organize the kitchen drawers. I throw away old stuff in the cabinets and closets. I decide to tackle the attic next.

I find my mother's wedding dress in a large white box with a ribbon attached. My heart jumps when I see it. I lift it, careful not to let it drop to the dusty floorboards. The dress has lace on top with pearls and sequins sewn in. The bottom has a full satin skirt. It looks tiny at the waist and gorgeous. Was Mom really this small? I examine the workmanship, so intricate and ornate. I love the delicate buttons up the back. I put it back in the box and carry it to my room.

There's not a decent mirror in the whole house. I wish I had a full-length mirror like in the dress shop Maura and I went to last week in Delaware. I see there is a hoop petticoat—so cool!—and I'll need someone to help me with all the buttons.

Even without the perfect mirror, I feel like the perfect bride when I put on this dress. I am going to wear this on my wedding day. Nothing will stop me. I feel like a fairy princess or a queen or a Hollywood bride. I want to show Mom how good I look.

Larry comes to dinner some nights when he doesn't have too much work to do. I make him things like pasta with basil pesto and Chicken Marsala. I want him to see what kind of wife I'll be. Dad and my sisters are there too, but I pretend we're alone at the table. I refill his glass and ask him about his day.

My car got the boot and I have to beg Dad to get the

money to pay off my fines. He says, "Why don't you ask Skippy?" Skippy is his joke name for Larry, and I don't like it. Dad can be mean like that. For instance, when I ran out of gas one night and called home, Dad said, "I can't deal with it right now. Why don't you call Skippy?"

That got me mad because I'm doing all sorts of things to help Dad. I got Mia on the pill. Dad didn't think it was a good idea, but the doctor agreed with me and so Dad caved. I put the pill with Mia's other pills.

I don't make a big deal about it, but if it keeps Mia from getting pregnant, it will be worth it. We've got enough stress around here without that.

I want to get married to get out of the house and get a fresh start on my own. Everyone says I'm too young, but I think they're wrong. I get frustrated with my family when they just hang around doing something dumb like sitting in the yard looking at Dad's new fish pond.

"How can you just sit there?" I ask Maura, "when there is so much work that needs to be done?"

"Take a chill pill, Meg," she says.

I think it's best not to think too much. If I drift off and think about Ruth, I get depressed and feel ashamed of myself. My healthy plans and patterns only last for part of a day or part of a week, but I can't consistently keep the promises I made to myself and to Ruth when I was in the hospital.

School is a priority for Dad, so I try to keep my grades up, but my heart isn't in it. I like some classes, but most seem irrelevant.

I want to do things, keep my mind occupied and my hands busy. I want to keep Mom's gardens going—nurture her perennials, especially her herb garden. Her flowers comfort me—her lilies, her roses, her peonies.

They give me more hours at Macy's. I get promotions, and they put me in charge of people older than me. I love learning all the aspects of the job, how it all fits together.

I can't keep still. If we have slow times, I start projects. I reorganize workspaces, display cases. I make neater schedules, and I leave notes to people who work on different shifts, so they can continue my work.

I have a friend named Daisy. She's a single mom with a great spirit. She makes me feel good and demands nothing of me. We laugh a lot and go out for drinks sometimes until she needs to pick up her daughter from daycare. She's my first black friend, and that feels very cool.

I like having friends who are busy. At home, I make breakfast for everyone and *forget* to eat myself. I keep bottles of Ensure around, just for show. I keep snacks and vitamins in the glove compartment. Sometimes I have to find a place to throw up. I throw up in alleys and trash cans if there's no bathroom around.

Larry and I go out to eat a lot. After each meal, and sometimes during, I excuse myself. I try to check to make sure the toilet flushes. I run the water in the sink for noise. I try to be quick about it.

Maura is my only nemesis. I feel her judgmental eyes on me all the time. She catches me trying on Mom's wedding dress. I stuff socks in the front of the dress for padding and she laughs.

"What do you think?" I ask.

"You look beautiful, but you don't need to stuff your bra," she says.

"Can you believe Mom was this size when she got

married? Here, help me with the buttons."

"Yeah, it is hard to believe she was ever this tiny," she says as she starts buttoning.

At the waistline, Maura starts to struggle getting the buttons done. "I don't want to tear the fabric. Maybe you should wait until you can find someone to alter the dress for you," she suggests.

"Are you saying I'm too fat to wear Mom's dress?" I yell, moving away.

"No, no. It's just old fabric and I don't want to rip it. I'm just saying you could get it altered so it's a perfect fit for *you*."

"Never mind. Just leave me alone."

I make a mental note to find somebody to restore the dress. I want to get Larry to set a wedding date. We graduate next May in 1984. I'm going to get all my credits in so I can graduate on time with Larry. So maybe next September I'll be a bride? That could work. Mom was 21 when she got married so why can't I? I'll focus my energy on this one event, like it's all that matters.

Maura
1983

I'm going to Hopkins
for graduate school. I'll trade
the quiet brick sidewalks of Chestertown
for the multi-colored row houses of Charles Village.

Right now, I'm searching the streets of Dublin
looking for my mother
and finding her in the pretty, plump faces
of the women who ride the bus
and tend to the bed and breakfasts.
She's in the green hills and the rebel songs.
She's climbing the Yeats Tower.

I send postcards home, extend my stay
for three weeks, cycle the Dingle Peninsula,
fall in love with an ex-con, drink Guinness
with my friend Cathy, and trust
the kindness of all the people who look like my relations.

None of this is the best part of the summer.

My dad picks me up at JFK
and on the way home
we stop for a night in Cape May.
Nothing is out of the way
for my dad. I get to stand on the beach
in New Jersey and realize that days before
I stood on Ireland's rocky coast at Lahinch

loving this same round moon.

Once I'm home, Dad stumbles off
to sleep and Mia is out with Danny, the new
boyfriend. The mood is light.
Meg is happy and bearing gifts:
champagne and cigarettes. The critical voice
in my head starts yapping, but I tell it
to shut up. What the hell,
my sister is here, and she wants to talk to me.

We celebrate my homecoming and my graduation
with laughter and champagne. The flying cork
attacks the stained-glass mallard duck on the kitchen
lampshade. The lamp clangs and sways. We fill
our glasses and laugh. We go into the backyard
and fill our lungs with poisonous cigarette smoke.
We laugh until we choke. We laugh
until our stories turn to tears. We say goodbye
to childhood. We crush the spent cigarettes with our heels
into the dirt of our backyard. We have crossed over
to a new place
where we don't have to
hate each other anymore.

Meg
1984

Maura is home from grad school, and it's my turn to finish school and start my real life.

Larry agreed we could get married in September. I caught him when he was in a good mood, after he had just gotten an A on his last final. Secretly, I'd been planning for this day forever, but now it was official. I asked Maura to be my maid of honor. Mindy and Mia and Daisy would be bridesmaids.

We were out trying on dresses when Maura asked me, "Are you still going to your counselor?"

"Sometimes," I say. "I don't make it every week."

"How about the food journal?"

"I'm not keeping it like I'm supposed to. After all, I am busy planning a wedding."

Maura looks at herself in the mirror and asks, "Do I really have to wear a bridesmaid's dress?"

"Only if you love me," I tell her.

"What if I only *like* you?" she says.

"You still have to wear the dress!" I say. "The dress looks good. Really. Don't you like the royal blue and the V-neckline?"

"It's not bad, but I never like the way I look. I want to start keeping a food journal," she says.

"You look beautiful," I tell her, and I mean it. I notice that she looks healthy. Her skin and hair are shiny. She's not slim, but she's not repulsive either. "Look at the little black beads at the neckline. You can use the black shoes you already have." I see her smile at me in the mirror. I like seeing her smile, and if the dress looks good on Maura, it will look good on the others, too.

Maura helps me all the time with the wedding chores. We practice making centerpieces with driftwood, shells, and candles. She asks about my therapy. I don't like lying to her.

To boost my spirits, I go visit Daisy and her daughter Claudia. Claudia is my flower girl, a precious little angel. Claudia is the only one who is as excited about the wedding as I am. She's going to wear a blue dress, a crown of white roses over her little cornrow braids, and delicate white gloves. It settles me to go over to Daisy's apartment and play dolls with Claudia.

Sometimes Dad and I fight over the reception menu. Maybe we won't have lobster, but I don't want the rubbery chicken either. I love looking at the long list of hors d'oeuvres, all the side dishes, the endless possibilities for the cake. Vanilla cream with raspberries? Mocha cream cheese? "Who's going to pay for all this?" Dad asks.

"We'll pay our part, and Larry's family will pay his part," I say.

Larry has wedding jobs he's supposed to do, but I have a hard time convincing him to do them. He can't be bothered to get fitted for the tux. He doesn't even know what a rehearsal dinner is until I tell him. I try to explain everything calmly, but I'm getting more and more excited as the date draws near. Some days I'm truly manic, but I want everything to be perfect.

I keep pressing Larry for details about the rehearsal dinner, but he keeps saying things like, "Well, it's a dinner, so I guess we'll eat." I give him my pouty face, but he just ignores me.

On the day before the wedding, I lay out my black and white jacket on the bed and find my pearls from Aunt Rachel. I drink a Bloody Mary while I do my hair. I'm taking my sisters and Daisy to the Glossy Glo Nail Bar to get our nails done. I feel a tremor of fear in my legs and I shake off a spell of dizziness. On this morning before my wedding, the angry yellow dragon starts breathing hot flames down my neck.

Maura
On the morning of September 13th

Meg takes us to the Fuzzy Navel
Hair Weave and Nail Bar.
It's not really called that.
I forget the name,
but it's in a part of the city
I don't know or feel comfortable in.
Will we find parking?
Daisy's brother owns the salon
so I try to bury my fear
when Meg turns on North Avenue,
a street I always avoid.
I have terrible nails anyway. It's just
one more form of bridesmaid torture
I shut up and endure.

I can tell Meg's been drinking
even though it's nine in the morning.
I bite my lip
and don't say a word. I don't want
to get on her bad side today.

The salon is a hoot. Daisy knows everyone
and we have fun getting beautified.
Jason is doing my nails, and he teases me,
"Let me do your toes," he says.
"No way, my feet are ticklish," I tell him.
I'm laughing and relaxed until
I see Meg drinking a glass of wine

and eating a cupcake. I think about
telling her to pace herself—she's driving
after all—but decide not to.
As we leave the salon, little Claudia arrives
with her grandmother.

Meg and Claudia run toward each other
on the sidewalk and crash for a big hello hug.
"Who's the cutest flower girl of all time?" says Meg.
Meg swings Claudia around and around
until one of Claudia's little shoes flies off
and lands in a bush. Mia goes off to retrieve the shoe.
After we say goodbye to Daisy's mother,
we pile into Meg's yellow Celica.
Daisy sits up front with Meg.
Mia, Claudia, and I are crammed in the back.
It's a tight squeeze,
and I can't see too well.
As we pull out,
someone beeps at us.
I wish, not for the first time,
that I had insisted on driving.
"Slow down, Meg!" I yell from the back.
"Oh, Maura, relax. I want to drive fast today.
It's my last day of freedom!"
Daisy says, "Go easy, Mario Andretti.
That's my baby in the back."
"*I'm* in the back, too," says Mia.
"You guys know I'd never do anything
to hurt you. What's next on our girl day
adventure?" says Meg.
"Just keep your eyes on the road, Meg," I say.

"Maura's an old party pooper, isn't she Claudia?"
says Meg. "Party pooper!" Claudia gleefully repeats.
"You got that right!" says Meg.
I feel a major headache coming on
and hope the next leg of our adventure
involves water and some aspirin.
Mia suggests McDonald's for fries,
but we can't think of one that's close
so we head straight to Daisy's place.
I feel a sigh of relief when we pull in
to the Silver Run apartments.
As soon as we enter, Meg heads straight
for the bathroom. That gives me a chance
to ask Daisy, "Do you think she's okay?"
"She's just excited about tomorrow,
I guess. Don't worry. We'll keep
an eye on her," Daisy says.
"I'm worried, though," I say.
"I wish I had driven instead."
"Don't fret. If you want, we can leave her car here,
and I'll drive y'all back home," Daisy says.
"Thanks," I say. "I think that would be better,
if you don't mind. She really didn't need to start
drinking wine first thing this morning," I say.
"She's one wild little thing, no doubt about it,"
says Daisy as Meg bursts into the room.
"What's for lunch?" Meg says.
"Is the thought of getting married
making you hungry?" Daisy laughs.
"Thirsty, really," Meg answers.
"Can you make me a blender drink?"
I shake my head and say, "Meg, seriously.

You shouldn't drink anymore.
You have the rehearsal and the dinner
to get through tonight," I remind her.
"That's exactly why I *need* a drink!" Meg says.
"Okay, honey," says Daisy,
"I'll make you a frozen Margarita,
light on the Tequila."
"Perfectamundo!" says Meg.
"At this rate, you're going
to need a nap before the dinner," I say.
 "Daisy," Meg asks, "can you explain why I chose
to spend today with Maura?"
I think I should call Dad
one minute
and that I'm completely overreacting
the next minute. I force myself to breathe
and I walk into Claudia's room. Claudia asks
if I want to see her special treasure.
She opens a small box and says,
"Meg says this is the most special treasure
of all time." When she lifts the lid,
I see a silver locket. "What picture
should I put inside?" Claudia asks.
"I'll take one of you at the wedding,"
Mia suggests. "I want my special people,"
Claudia says. "Take one of Mommy and take one
of Meg in her wedding dress."
"Good idea," I say,
"You're one of Meg's special people, too," I tell Claudia.
"I'm her *very* favorite," Claudia tells us.

In the living room, Meg is looking

for a third Supreme to join in a rendition
of "Stop! In the Name of Love." Claudia and Mia
start singing at the top of their lungs.
I'm disgusted with the whole bunch of them.

I look at the clock. In four hours,
we need to be in the church
for the rehearsal. When they reprise,
"You Can't Hurry Love" for the fourth time,
I slip into Daisy's bedroom to call Dad.
He doesn't pick up.
I don't know Larry's number.
I say a quick prayer.

"What's next?" I hear Meg yell.
"What do you want to sing, Maura?" Meg asks.
"Nothing," I tell her. "I'm not in the mood."
Meg starts trying to belt out the Glenn Miller song:
"In the mood...I think I've got it...In the mood...
Can someone help me?...I don't know the words,
but I am...in the mood now..." Meg sings.
I'm being moody in the kitchen thinking about
how to sneak Meg's car keys away from her.
"Wait, I've got a great one for you, Maura. The Beatles."
Meg shuffles through albums until she finds what she
     wants.
"Daisy, you have the best vinyl! Maura, this our perfect
     theme
for today," says Meg. And she starts to play "Hello,
     Goodbye."
"Come on, everybody. We're singing this one for Maura.
Meg starts singing with the Beatles, *"You say*

yes. I say no. You say stop. I say go go go.
Oh, no! You say goodbye,
and I say hello.
Hello, hello.
I don't know why you say goodbye, I say hello."
The song continues, and everyone is in a party mood
except for me.
I can't stop thinking about what I need to do,
but I don't *know* what to do. I just know I'm
missing all the fun. Again.

I go into the bathroom when I feel like
I'm about to cry. That's when I notice the music
has stopped. I walk into the living room.
Meg is hunting for her purse.
"Hey, Meg. Give me your keys," I say,
"I'm driving us home."
"No way, Maura,
I'm absolutely fine! You're spoiling my fun!"
"Just wait, Meg. Let me get Mia."
I race to tell Mia we're leaving,
but when I get back to the living room,
the door is open, and Meg is gone.

We leave the main door of the apartment building
in time to see Meg sashaying down the sidewalk.
Her hair is swinging, and her hips are swinging
as if she can still hear the music in her head.
I call out to her, but she doesn't turn.
She keeps walking full steam
until she comes to the steps.

From the top of the steps, I see
Meg sprawled at the bottom—
not moving, not crying, just lying there
looking broken. Daisy sees me, and I yell
back to her, "Call 911!"
"Oh, no!" Mia cries.
Meg is restless, but not alert.
She whimpers and moans
like she's having bad dreams.
I think she must have hit her head,
but I don't see any blood.
I don't want to move her.

We wait thirty-seven minutes, but it seems like hours.
Random thoughts swirl through my mind.
Is there something I should be doing?
Meg cries out,
but she doesn't respond when I talk to her.
I look down at our painted nails.
Mine look smudged, but hers
still look perfect.

I hear a siren. There are two strong men,
young and agile. Efficient and gentle.
They talk about vitals and multiple fractures.
They ask a few questions. Mia's sobs have
turned to hiccups. I can tell she wants to flirt
with the EMTs.
They are doing their job.
My mind is racing. There is something
I should be doing. I call out,
"Where are you taking her?"

"Immanuel Hospital," they say
as they slam the doors.

Mia and I follow the ambulance
downtown to the hospital.
I worry about parking. I don't know what I'm doing.
I'm not used to Meg's car. Mia keeps asking
questions I can't answer: *Is Meggie alright?*
What happens now? Do I still get
to go to Diamonte's for dinner? Are Meg
and Larry still getting married tomorrow?
I try to keep my cool. I feel close
to hitting Mia and my words to her
are harsh. I have to remind myself
to keep breathing. I pass the hospital
three times before I find
the parking lot entrance. Each minute it takes
us to get there is another minute
Meg is left alone.

We find the emergency room,
but we're no closer to seeing Meg
or knowing what's going on. We wait
in line to talk to someone, and then
we wait some more. The atmosphere
is hectic. No one can even confirm for us
that she arrived. An older man is holding
bloody bandages on his arm.
Mia and I can't find two seats together,
which is fine with me.

Meg

The sky grows dark and balls of ice swirl in the sky. I run and run. At first, I feel firm wet sand under my feet, then firm hot sand, then loose, deep sand, then hot sand blowing in my eyes, and I can't run any more. My legs give way and I fall. An electric pain jolts me. Am I having a seizure? I feel like I'm on fire, but I don't see any flames.

I'm in the sandstorm, and I can't feel anything, but I continue to feel the heat, the scorching pain, the blinding, shooting pain. I'm lifted or blown by the hot wind and a pattern emerges before my eyes, a pattern in gold and copper tones. It looks like a tapestry.

Then fear replaces pain as my dominant impression. I know where I am. I've seen this creature before—the yellow dragon. I am afraid, but I'm mesmerized by its beauty—a creature so immense and so near, so appealing, and yet so terrifying.

Through the sand, I see it fly, rising in a torrent of wings. A stench in the air makes me gag. I nearly suffocate and then seconds later, I can breathe again. Something sharp lands a blow that shakes my whole body. I see the creature lift from the ground, serpent-like, but graceful in flight. The dragon has power; it owns me.

Blisters form on my hands and arms—angry, red blisters. I know I must run, but my legs won't move. I try to stand and cannot. The wind fills my mouth, and I close my eyes against the assault.

I feel myself curl into a ball, waiting for the death blow. I feel the breath of the dragon, burning away what's left of me.

Time passes this way. I sleep or lose consciousness,

unable to help myself. I become aware of the sound of flutes, a clear sound that begs me not to sleep. That's when I feel myself being lifted from the ground. Strong arms carry me. I fight an urge to sleep and will my eyes to open. I see a familiar blue shirt. Larry is here to rescue me.

Maura

I don't recognize Dad right away
when he walks through the emergency room doors.
He's wearing a gray suit, dressed for the rehearsal dinner
he's supposed to be attending.
I feel relief when I see him. Mia rushes over.
"What happened?" Dad asks.
"Meg fell down the stairs," Mia says.
I shrug. "We don't know anything yet,"
I say. Dad walks to the counter and starts
trying to charm a nurse into giving him some information.
I go back to sit, glad not
to be in charge anymore. Then Larry
walks through the door and I wonder
what I'll say to him. He stands still for a moment
running a hand through his sandy curls.
Mia launches herself on him, and I turn away.
I see Dad approach Larry. Mia sobs and hangs
her arm awkwardly around Larry's neck.
I hear Dad say, "She's here, but that's all
they'll say. It looks like she has multiple fractures
from the fall."
"She wouldn't have fallen
if she hadn't been drinking all day."
I blurt it out, not meaning to.
I can't believe I just said that, and from the look
on their faces, they can't believe it either.
Even Mia stops her fake crying
and we stand there in a silent circle.
"Let's all sit down over here," says Dad.
The crowd has started to thin

and we find seats. "What's going on?"
Dad asks.
"Just what I said. Meg's been drinking
since breakfast. I tried to get her to stop, but she wouldn't
    listen
and she just fell down those concrete steps
and didn't get up. She's falling apart, Dad. She's drinking
too much and she's not going to the therapist. She needs
help, and not just from broken bones."
Mia gets a stricken look on her face and asks,
"Is Meg going to die?"
"No, no, Mia," says Dad. "Now let's everybody just calm
    down
here a minute. We have to take care of one problem at a
    time."
"I think her problems are connected, Dad. I don't think
it's going to work to take them one at a time," I say.
I look over at Larry and think, *welcome to the family.*
I can see how uncomfortable he looks, but his opinion
seems crucial, so I ask, "Larry, do you see any of this?"
He sits there for a while before speaking. In fact,
I don't think he is going to speak,
when he finally says, in a whisper,
"She needs more help than I can give her."

Meg

I hear someone calling me and shining a bright light in my face. It might be my mother. "Mom, is it you?" I want to say. I think I say it, but I don't. I can't say anything.

I feel people moving me. I feel cold air on my arms and legs. I hear the rattle of metal, and carts rolling across the floor. I feel people stretching me out like they are going to tie me to a rack. Sometimes the room is light, and sometimes the room is dark. They are wrapping me up like I'm a mummy. There is nothing I can do about any of this. I would scream if I could find the energy to do it. Instead all I can do is exist like a cloud that floats in the sky or a leaf that floats away in a stream.

Maura

Outside, the sky darkens. We are in
for a long night. Dad pulls his tie off
and shoves it in his pocket. A doctor finally
approaches and tells us Meg has been admitted
and she's in the ICU. He asks us to follow him
and we do. The clock on the wall says seven o'clock.
We're supposed to be eating dinner at Diamonte's
Italian Garden right now. I haven't eaten since breakfast
and my stomach grumbles at the thought.

A man in black pants and a white shirt
introduces himself as Megan's intake counselor
and asks to have a word with the parents. "I'm her Dad,
and this is her fiancé, Larry, and these are her sisters,
Maura and Mia."
"Larry and Meg are getting married tomorrow," says
        Mia.
"Is that so?" the counselor says. "Well, if you could all
        follow me."
"When will we get to see Meg?" I ask.
"As soon as I get some information from you," he says,
"I'll page the doctor."
We follow as we're told, but then
we're left to wait again.
Larry says, "I should call my mother.
She's probably freaking out."
"At least Daisy can let her know it was a real
emergency that canceled the dinner. I should call
Father Ryan, too, and let him know. He can say a prayer
for Meg, and maybe he'll even visit," I say.

"Meg will be all better by tomorrow," Mia says.

The guy comes back with his clipboard. He says,
"I'm sorry for the delay," and sits down.
"The doctors have made some discoveries
they wanted me to share with you. I had already
gone home for the day when they called me back in."
"Megan had an extremely high blood alcohol level
when she was admitted. It's consistent with what we see
in cases of alcohol poisoning. It's a life-threatening
   condition,
obviously. In addition to that, she may have suffered a
   blow
to the head when she fell, and she has multiple severe
   fractures
on the right side of her body in her right leg and hand.
   Right now,
we have her on fluids and oxygen, and we are keeping
her vital signs monitored. She seems to have
a weakened state of overall health. Is there anything
you could share about her health in general?"
"Well, she's currently being treated as an outpatient
for an eating disorder," says Dad.
The counselor says, "My professional opinion
is that she may be suffering
from multiple disorders at this point,
but don't lose heart.
She got here in time today, and our job now
is to come up with a plan to save her life."

Meg

On September 14th, the day I am supposed to be married, they tell me I need a 12-Step Alcohol Detox and Recovery Program. The team has other recommendations. I'm not well enough yet to be moved.

Once I'm stable, I'll get more treatment for the eating disorder.

They use the word *alcoholism*, which doesn't make sense. Are they really talking about me or do they mean someone else? I want to climb out of the bed and say, *You're wrong. There's been a mistake*, but I can't move without pain, and I can't put any words together. When Daddy holds my hand, I relax a little. Why are all these people in my room?

Maura

When does a drink
to unwind
become a flood
that washes away
your whole life?
I think back to the best
day I ever spent with Meg
--the day she made a Homecoming
surprise and we drank
champagne. Would the conversation
have even happened
without the sparkling wine?
Can Meg learn
to do without alcohol
forever? Could I?
Meg's case manager,
Joshua Cross, says, "You're not
going to get all the answers
to your questions today. That's why
they call it a 12-Step process;
you must take things
one step at a time.
I want to help Meg.
I want to help myself.
Is there such a thing
as family, food, and alcohol
therapy? I wonder
what Mom would say
about all this.

Meg

I wake up and wonder where I am. I know I'm in big trouble. Plastic tubing is taped to my face and my left arm. My body feels like it's wrapped in gauze. My head could explode any minute.

"You're a very lucky young lady," some fool says at my bedside.

He's young and kind of cute, I think. My doctor?

"How so?" I manage to croak.

"Well, we weren't sure you were going to make it through the night," he says. "But here you are today, and you're doing better."

Everyone talks like this. *Near fatal alcohol levels*, they say. *Permanent damage to my bones. Malnutrition and dehydration. Anemia and nutrient deficiencies. I'm out of chances, out of time.*

They list the things I need to do to survive, *if I want to survive*, they say. The list is long: detox, treatment, education, counseling.

I'll always be in recovery, they say. Abstinence from alcohol is my only option.

Do I want to live? People I know—Dad, Maura, Mia, and Larry—and people I don't know, all ganging up on me: *do I want to live?*

I guess I say yes. They roll me down the hall and put me in an ambulance. For the briefest moment, I feel the sun on my face, feel its warmth. I take a cold and bumpy ride to a residential treatment center. I'm pretty sure I'm sedated. I won't be able to see or talk to my family. Dad said, "We'll come to see you as soon as we can."

Maura

Every day I pray
Meg's fragile little body
will make it through detox.

Meg

They say it's best I don't know where I am. The first stage of recovery will be lonely, they say.

And hellish, they should say, but don't. I shake like a girl with her finger in a light socket. My bones are broken. I'm rags and bones. My teeth rattle in my head. So cold, so cold. They put a hand-knitted green cap on my head. They cover me with heated blankets. I can never get warm.

When I pass by a mirror, I don't recognize myself. I try to use my left hand, but it doesn't work. There are crusty places on my face. Everything hurts or itches. The sounds that come out of me are frightening, more wild beast than human. I scream when they touch me. I scream from fear, and I scream from pain.

Sometimes, in my delirium, an image comes to me: warm arms carrying me, a soft blue shirt against my face. I don't get to see Larry, but he's the one who carries me, carries me away from the yellow dragon. When I think of him, I can relax and sleep. Sleep is about the only comfort I have, until the nightmares start and then I realize, there is no comfort at all.

One morning, someone leaves a notebook and a pen on my table. I can't write with my right hand, but I try. My writing looks like a first grader's, so I draw flowers and vines instead.

I start counting, like a person stranded on a deserted island scratching marks on a palm tree. How long have I been here? I count the hours until I can get pain meds. I count the days. I count the bites it takes me to eat a muffin. I count eight glasses of water. Do I want to live enough to count my blessings?

My counselor's name is Aleta Melicor. I ask her, "How do I change?"

She answers, "Become something new." She tells me to start each day with the ritual of putting on a piece of clothing like I am putting on the new me. Hokey and ridiculous, I think, but really, I don't have a better idea. Every day, I start putting on my garment of salvation, one difficult sleeve at a time.

Maura

All I can do
is worry and obsess about
my mother, about my sister.
I miss them both as if my body
is functioning in the world
without some vital organ.
I feel as powerless to help Meg
as I am powerless
to bring my mother back.

I go to the graduate poetry workshop
and hate all the poems, especially
my own. I can't wait to leave and go
back to my apartment so I can
lie on my back on the floor by the window.
It hurts less to lie quietly in the sun
reminding myself to breathe.

Everybody in the workshop smokes,
so I start smoking, too,
in self-defense. I search through all Mom's
letters looking for the ones
where she mentions Meg. I can't stop
reading them. I get to see
Meg for the first time this weekend.
Will I take this letter?

March 15, 1980

Dear Maura,

Happy news! I found the perfect pattern for Meg's senior prom gown. It's so dear, and she will look beautiful in it. I'm also making a little purse from the same material, and I'm going to crochet a pink shawl for her shoulders. Larry is such a nice boy, and I think he is a good influence. She doesn't seem as keen on him as she was on Mark, but that's life.

She and I did have a nice talk this evening. I was afraid to show her the pattern for fear that she'd hate it and we'd have another blowout. But believe it or not, she loved the dress and even seemed appreciative of the effort I'm going to for her. Wonders never cease.

Just had time to say a quick hello and thought you would like to know your sister and I had one evening of peace.

Don't work too hard. I love you and can't wait until we're all together again at Easter.

Love always,
Mom

Meg

On Day 13, I fall to pieces. All at once, I realize what I've done to myself and an avalanche of negative emotions crushes me. How will I fix everything I've broken?

I'm sick, alone, and sending my dad into the poorhouse with every day that I stay at this resort for rejects. Rest Haven. It sounds like the name of an old age home or a mortuary. It's a place for losers, and I fit right in.

Every single action is a struggle.

I still can't do very much on my own. I should be a happy newlywed right now, but instead, I'm here *alone*, in a wheelchair, forced to eat, forced to drink water.

Trips to the bathroom are like climbing Mt. Everest. First, there's the pain of moving because everything hurts. Next, there's the complete lack of privacy. My every bodily function is watched, recorded, and analyzed.

Misery is my only companion. It distracts me from the total mess I've made of my life. I whine about my physical ailments. I shiver and shake. I wear my green cap night and day. Before, I wouldn't be caught dead looking like this, but who cares now?

Somehow, I pull things together during the day. I go to my meals and my counseling. I read what they tell me to read and write what they tell me to write. But the nights are scary. I either can't sleep at all or I have nightmares that wake me in a panic.

Rolling into my group session on Day 13, I must look like a clown. I'm in there with a bunch of talkers, so I'm used to just sitting there and passing the time until they let me out. I listen to one pathetic sob story after another. As a species, human beings are messed up.

I count the minutes until I can leave. I watch the clock.

A lean, long-haired guy named Rob leads the group. He rambles on for several minutes. Then I notice everyone is staring at me.

"Meg?" Rob asks.

"I'm sorry. What did you say?" I ask back.

"I asked what you think of our quote of the day," says Rob.

"Oh," I say. "I didn't really hear what that was."

Rob points, and I look up at the board and see this: *Your most important relationship is with yourself.* Makes me barf, I think. "Sounds like Shakespeare to me," is what I say aloud. Nobody laughs.

"What do you think it means, Meg?" Rob continues.

I'm at my breaking point. "Look, I don't know what it means, and I don't care what it means. I'm just trying to survive here."

"I think it means we need to be true to ourselves," Heather offers. Heather is always so helpful.

"Thanks, Heather. Meg brings up the issue of survival. Some of us have been where she is today. Is there any connection between survival and relationships?" Rob keeps looking right at me.

"I don't know what you want me to say," I tell him. "That I've ruined every relationship I ever had? How is that supposed to help?" I want to know.

"The quotes are meant to get us talking. We can't keep our emotions bottled up or we'll explode. Do you want to talk about the relationships you think you've ruined, Meg?"

"Maybe we should talk about all the people who *aren't* going to come to visit me this Sunday: my ex-fiancé, my dad who won't look me in the face, my dead mother—take your pick," I yell across the room.

"Who do you want to talk about?" Rob says, still looking only at me.

After an awkward silence, Heather says meekly, "I'd like to talk about my boyfriend, if that's okay."

Finally, Rob stops staring at me and lets Heather drone on and on. At the end of group, I almost make it out the door, but Rob stops me.

"Do you want to take a walk?" he asks.

"Yeah, right," I say, looking at the wheelchair.

"You know what I mean," Rob says.

"Like I ever have a choice around this place," I say.

"You *do* have a choice, Meg," Rob says. "In fact, the choices you make in this next year will mean the difference between life and death. I'm not trying to be dramatic or anything, but there are just some facts to consider. For someone in your situation, there's about a 60% chance you'll make it through the next year without taking a drink. If you can do that, you have a chance for a normal life, but it's all about your choices."

"I just don't have the energy to think about all this right now."

"Well, then you can choose to give up... in which case, you'll probably be dead in a year."

"Maybe I'll come back in a year, just to prove I'm not dead," I tell him.

"I don't like to see people come back here unless you want to come back to help. That's what I did. I got help; now, I want to help other people."

"What if I'm just a hopeless case?" I wonder aloud.

"We're all hopeless cases without a little help from our

friends," he says.

I think, *this guy is just a walking cliché.* "Isn't that a Beatles song?" I say.

"Meg, you're good at changing the topic, but really, you have these six weeks to get your life on track. If you don't do the hard work now, the stats say you aren't going to make it."

"None of this stuff is going to help me. Why do they think that talking about some lame quotation is going to help?"

"Well, I'm the lame one who picked the quote, so thanks a lot."

"I'm sorry, but 'Your most important relationship is with yourself'? Tell me, how is that going to help me?"

"There's this unwritten rule that you shouldn't start a long-term relationship with anyone until you've had a full year of sobriety. The idea is you have to work on yourself first before you can handle the emotions of a relationship. I just thought it was worth discussing, and correct me if I'm wrong, but I think it hit a nerve with you."

"How come you're being so nice to me?" I ask him.

"Well, it's my job. Plus, I guess I feel sorry for you with all the casts and the wheelchair. It's hard enough to get motivated to change without a bunch of broken bones to deal with."

"Did they tell you I did this on the day before I was supposed to get married?"

"I heard something about that. Yeah. That's really messed up," he says, and I can tell he's fighting back a laugh.

"Tell me: what am I supposed to do about a relationship I'm already in? Just tell him, meet me in a year when I'm clean and sober?"

"Have you talked to him yet?"

"Not alone. He was there when they did the intervention thing at the hospital."

"Maybe he'll be patient. You seem to me like someone worth waiting for."

I look at Rob, with his flannel shirt and moppy hair. For once, I don't give a smart-ass reply. Instead, I say, "Thanks, I needed to hear that."

Things get a little easier after that. I even start listening and participating in group. One day, I throw the little green cap in the trash and ask if I can get help washing my hair.

In group sessions, Rob walks us through the steps. The first step is to admit you have a problem. I have to admit to multiple problems and put it in writing.

One day, Rob asks the group, "How do you all feel about the higher power stuff? Some people don't buy in to that."

The discussion is interesting, and I hear myself saying, "I believe in God, but will God restore me to sanity? I don't know."

There's a big debate in the group about the idea of powerlessness. Are we powerless or do we have a choice? It all makes my head hurt, but it's fascinating. I have to admit, I've never thought about any of this stuff before.

On chilly afternoons after group, Rob and I sometimes "walk" together. I tell him things I haven't told Aleta, my real counselor. I admit to him, "I know if I leave here today, I would probably go back to the same behaviors that put me here. I'm afraid I'm just going to keep doing these things until I kill myself. The world is just too full of temptation. How do you make yourself do the right thing when no one's watching?"

"I won't sugar coat it. It's hard. For me, I have to visualize a big poison sticker on every bottle of alcohol; but that's what alcohol is for me—poison. And I stay away from family and friends who have a lifestyle that involves drinking. That's why it helps to have friends who are going through recovery with you. You can talk when you feel tempted. They can help you remember what's at stake."

We stop talking, and I feel warm sunlight on my arm. Yellow leaves are all over the ground. "Just leave me here. I need to think," I tell Rob.

"I'm not supposed to, but I guess it'll be okay for a few minutes. Can you handle the chair by yourself?" he asks.

"I'm okay. It's slow-going, but I think I can make it."

"Yes. I think you can," he says.

I watch leaves blow across the sidewalk. I think about Mom. Not so long ago she was alive, and I was a normal college kid. I think about my friend Ruth Carson. I don't want my story to end that way.

As I roll myself back inside, I think, *heck, if someone like Rob can do it, I can too.*

Maura

I visit Meg on Sunday.
It's a long drive to the western part
of Maryland. I drive up steep
inclines and wonder if Nana's car
is going to make it.

I hope I'll say the right thing.

Even after you drive through
Rest Haven's gate, it's a long way
to the actual building
where Meg lives. It's pretty, though.
Maybe I'll write
a poem about this day.

"You look well," I tell her.
"I didn't know what to expect,
how do you feel? I'm sorry.
I'm talking too much."

"It's okay," she says,
looking childlike and small, but otherwise
fine. Her hair is shiny and glows
a pale yellow.

"So how are you feeling?"
I try again.

"Better—some bad days,
some worse nights.

I'm hanging in," she says.
"I guess everybody's talking
about me."

"It's not like that. People
are concerned, but I'm at school,
so I don't hear much," I say.
I tell her I talk to Daisy. That Marge
from Macy's called. I tell about all
the cards people are sending.
"I brought them for you," I say,
and give her the cards, plus the one card
from Mom I want her to read. They are tied
together in a red ribbon.

"Thanks," she says,
taking the stack of cards and letters.
"How are Dad and Mia?
Thanks for not bringing her,
by the way."

"They're doing all right, I guess."
We'll all be doing better
when you are, I think,
but don't say.
"Are you eating?" I say,
and then immediately regret it.

"Yes, I'm *eating*," Meg says with a hard edge
to her voice, and then she adds,
"I'm sorry. None of this is easy.
I can't understand

why I did this to myself."

"Isn't it the job of these people
to help you understand?" I ask.

"They think it's their job
to make my life a living hell," she says.

"I'm sorry you have to go through this.
They made it sound in the hospital
like this was the best place around.
We didn't know what to do.
We just had to take their word for it."

"Have you talked to Larry? Do you know
if he ever plans to come see me?" she asks.

"After the hospital," I say, "he sort of disappeared.
I didn't see him at church
on the day you two were supposed to get married.
Everybody's asking how he is,
but I haven't wanted to bother him."

"I haven't heard from him either.
He probably hates me, and I don't blame him," she says.

"I'm sure that's not true,
but he was shocked and overwhelmed at the hospital,
like we all were. We didn't know
what was happening. No one would tell us
anything. I think it was three in the morning
before they let Dad see you. It was awful," I tell her.

"God, this whole thing is so embarrassing.
How am I ever going to face anyone?" she asks.

"Don't be embarrassed. Just get well.
That's all anybody wants. What can I do to help you?"

"I don't know, Maura. I wish I knew."
"Is there anything I can bring? I think Dad
will bring Mia next week," I say.

"I'm not sure I can deal with that."

"I know what you mean. All she can talk about
is how she missed her chance to be a bridesmaid
till I'm about ready to strangle her. I know she's trying
to deal with this too, but her tears just seem
so fake and phony. She can turn on the tears
like a switch if anybody calls or visits."

"Well, if she comes, she better stay quiet."
"You know she won't," I say.
"Then maybe you can tell Dad to stay home
for the time being," Meg says.
"Is all this helping, do you think?" I ask her.

"How do I know? I can't do anything wrong here.
They watch me like I'm a criminal."

"Well," I say, "it's just got to work
and that's all there is to it. I can't do without you,"
I say, and then I break down a little.

When I recover, I continue, "They told us you have
six weeks here, and then ninety days follow-up, at least."

"What a nightmare. How is Dad paying for this?" Meg
    asks.

"Don't worry about that. I think it's mostly covered
by insurance, and we'll figure out the rest," I tell her.

"I know it's expensive," she says. "One day I was
    complaining
and being my usual bitchy self and this one nurse told me
I could just *get out* if I didn't want to cooperate. People
    were lined
up at the door, she said, and I'd better just appreciate the
    sacrifices
my family was making so I could be here. That's how she
    put it—
the sacrifices my family was making."

"I don't know how much it costs, but I do know
we had to get special permission
to send you here because there were
people on a waiting list."

"I guess the whole world's screwed up," she says.

"Well, we aren't the only family
that needs a place like this, that's for sure."

"I just want to know how Larry's feeling," she says.

"I wouldn't try to guess," I say. "He'll let you know. He's just giving you some time. That's what the doctor told us to do," I tell her.

"It's just, there are things I want to tell him, things I wish I'd already told him."

"There will be time for that, I'm sure," I tell her. "I'm not so sure," Meg says. "I'm not sure about anything."

Meg

Just like that, one Sunday, there he is, right in front of me. His curls are longer and untidy, but he is still my Larry. He wears a grungy-looking shirt and jeans. I'm sitting in the glass room, at least that's what they call it. It's a big room with lots of windows and it's a perfect place to sit and watch the autumn leaves. I'm writing in my journal when he walks in and I look twice to make sure it's really him.

I look him in the eyes. "You hate me," I say—a statement, not a question.

I've never seen him look so uncomfortable. He almost nods but then says, "Of course not." He looks hurt and puzzled, and then we do the only thing we can do—we laugh.

"I don't blame you for hating me. I hate myself for what I did," I say.

"I don't hate you, Meg. Even in here, you're still the most beautiful girl I've ever seen, but that's why I was so afraid to see you. I feel like you always make me end up doing something I don't want to do."

"Well, you're off the hook now. I don't want anything from you," I say.

"That's what you say now, but in a minute, you'll have me trying to break you out of this place." That makes me smile for first time.

"You'd really do that for me?" I say, faking a southern accent.

"I'm not falling into that one. No way am I answering that question," he says, but that breaks the ice, and I give him a big hug.

"Not to worry. We're not going to turn into the Bonnie and Clyde of Alcohol Detox. I'm just glad you finally came to see me. I've missed you," I tell him.

"I don't really know yet how I feel about things...about us. I can't make any promises today. I *mean* it," Larry says, trying to convince himself, I guess.

"I don't want any promises from you. In fact, I just want to tell you one thing: you're my hero," I say.

"Now don't start. Don't flatter me," he says.

"You saved me. You're my hero," I repeat.

"I don't know what you're talking about, Meg, and I don't want to know," he says.

"I was being eaten by a big, scary, fire-breathing dragon and you rescued me," I continue.

"I guess this was a dream?" he asks.

"I guess it was a dream, but it seemed so real, so much more real than anything else that has happened to me lately," I say. "I was running, and I was trapped, and I was a goner, but you just swooped in and carried me to safety."

I reach up and touch his curls, put my arms around his neck. He is not hugging back, but I keep on holding on. "I know this sounds weird, but I want you to know that I know it was you who saved me. And when that happened, I knew I completely loved you with my whole heart."

"Meg, I didn't save you from anything."

"Well, somebody did," I say, "and he was wearing your shirt!"

"Can we be serious, Meg?" he says, and breaks away from me. "I didn't want to say it like this, but I have to tell you something. I'm going to California. I wasn't sure I could tell you, but I have to do this. *Please* let me do this." His eyes have this puppy dog pleading look in them.

I'm in shock. "So, you're telling me now that we're just completely finished? Is that what you're saying? Instead of that 'love, honor, and trust' stuff we *almost* said to each other, you're just leaving me, right now, for good?"

"See, Meg. This is why I didn't want to come here. I have this idea in my head of what I think is right for me, and you have an idea in your head of what's right for you, and they just don't match. I have to go to California to check out this film program. I'd like you to tell me it's *okay* with you if I go."

"You obviously don't need my permission, and it's not like I can chase after you. You can do what you want." I say.

"I'm so sorry, Meg. I'm sorry that I didn't tell you how I felt before, and I'm sorry that I couldn't help you before things got...so out of control. And now, I just need a break from all this..." he says.

I see his pain, and I realize I have power here. I can *choose* to make him feel like shit, or for once, I can listen to what he wants, what he needs.

I tell him, "Larry, I'm glad you came to see me. I'm glad you told me. It's okay, really. I hope you find what you're looking for out there."

Before he leaves, we cry, we hold hands. He says, "We should have known it would never work when you fell asleep during *The Empire Strikes Back*."

We laugh some more. I like this new Larry. It takes all my strength, but I don't try to make him feel guilty or try to change his mind.

I tell him I love him one more time, and then I let him go.

Maura

On Sunday night, Dad tells me
he drove all the way out to Rest Haven
and couldn't turn in the driveway.

He's losing it, I think. I try
to talk to him about the serious changes
we need to make as a family
but he just changes the subject or makes a joke.

Without Meg, he has to make sure
Mia takes her pills. He has to pay
the bills. "This is serious," I tell him.
"We have to get rid
of all the liquor in the house."

"You're being ridiculous,"
is his response. I tell him,
"I'm not making this up. That's what
they said to do at the Al-Anon meeting.
You could come to those, too. They help."
"They just help somebody to make a buck
is all they do," Dad says.
"It's not that way at all, Dad.
They are just people like us,
learning to cope with the disease
of alcoholism. It's a *disease,* Dad."
"We don't need to worry about all that,"
Dad says. "Meg is just under
a little stress. She's going to be just fine."
I keep trying. I say,

"She's an alcoholic, Dad...and I think
Mom may have been one, too."
"Now you leave your mother out of it!"
he says, raising his voice, which he
rarely does. I try again,
"Dad, I'm not trying to upset you,
but I'm learning a lot, and alcoholism
is *hereditary*. It's something *our family*
needs to figure out
so we can support Meg. Denying
that we have a problem
is not going to help her."
"We'll do what we can to help
your sister, Maura, but there's no way
I'm throwing all the booze away...
In fact, this whole conversation
is making me thirsty. I think
I'm going out for a little while."

Father Ryan says that in situations like this
I need to learn
to listen to Dad
with my eyes.
The priest tells me,
"Watch what he *does*, rather than
listen to his words.

And sure enough,
when I come home the next weekend,
the entire liquor cabinet is empty
except for the pewter cups
Mom filled every night

with crushed ice and Scotch
and a twist of lemon.

Meg

I'm learning things here without the distractions of real life. I feel better after I write. Writing is a cure for me, which feels like something important. And ha! Even my dad wrote me a letter. Here's what I found in my mail slot this morning:

Dear Meg,

I can't believe I've started this letter three times. Writing comes easy to you, but not to your 'ole dad. I've spent a lot of time lately thinking about you girls when you were little. That seems like such an easy time compared to now.

I drove over to see you last Sunday, but I couldn't pull in. I guess Maura told you. I just kept driving, then turned around and came home. I don't want you to think I didn't visit because I don't care, but I just couldn't bear to see you in that place again. You'll always be my little Meg, and it hurts too much to see you with those casts, looking so pale. I've met Father Ryan a few times. Your name is on a prayer card or some such thing. I guess our family is keeping those old nuns busy.

You might like to know I paid all the bills this morning, so things should be good for another month. I've been setting out Mia's pills like you taught me. She's happy with some new boyfriend. I lose track of all their names.

Your doctor hasn't told me yet, but someday soon, I'm going to pick you up and take you to the new place he

*wants to send you. I'm proud of you for sticking with all
this. You're a smart cookie, and you'll figure it out.*

*Sorry it takes a letter for me to say this, but I really love
you, Meg. I'll sure be happy to see you at home again, but
I guess we have to leave it to the experts to tell us when
that's gonna be.*

Take good care,
Dad

I read the letter three times and then look at my glass
of orange juice. At home, I would sneak some vodka in
there to help me deal with all the emotions this letter
makes me feel, but here I am: alone with myself and my
healthy Florida orange juice. I take a small sip. It's
horrible, really—bland and tasteless. Is this what my life
has become?

Dad calls me his little girl and a smart cookie. I can't
let him down. Yet, if I give up my *spicy* life, am I giving up
who I am?

It's my moment of truth, and I see a small window of
opportunity here. I'm starting to believe in the cocktail of
clichés they keep feeding me: *you can do it, one day at a
time.*

They tell me I'm ready, but I don't feel ready. I need a
sponsor, someone who will hold me accountable. I think
of Ruth, and I get angry. Why was she all alone in the
hospital? Had she been abandoned by everyone or did she
isolate herself? Why wasn't she here to help me now? Why
did she wait until it was too late to be saved? The questions
buzz in my head, but they don't get me anywhere.

I lift my fork. The eggs are cold. I try a potato. Then another one. I taste seasoned salt and think of Mom. If I close my eyes, I can imagine her in the kitchen.

I cover my eggs with a napkin and focus on the potatoes. I breathe. I eat the strawberry and the little bit of cantaloupe and even the mint garnish. Life is delicious.

"I can't do the eggs," I tell Marla.

"It's okay, honey. You did pretty good today," she tells me.

I feel a very slight fullness inside of me, a light and lemony kind of energy. I feel stronger—even younger, if that makes any sense—than I did a week ago.

I can't do the exercise class yet, but I can take a sauna. I like to feel warm. Then I practice walking with crutches until group starts.

Maura

Meg is zen-like and peaceful.
It's freaky. She tells me about Larry
leaving for California almost as if she's describing
someone else's life and not her own.
I wonder if they have her on mood-
altering drugs. We are walking through
"the valley of the shadow of death,"
but just like in the psalm
we fear no evil. Life falls into a pattern
of coping with pain
and trying to do what's right. The pain
doesn't go away, but the love
doesn't either. Whatever our parents did
or didn't do right, they at least
taught us how to love each other.
That loves shows at Meg's
homecoming celebration. I get rid
of every drop of alcohol in the house
including mouthwash and vanilla extract.
Most of it, I pour down the sink.
We drink sparkling water with splashes
of lime and apple cider. We make cheese fondue
in Mom's orange fondue pot. We three sisters
even pass a cigarette among us in the backyard
because, as Meg says, "Shit, we can't give up
everything all at once." Because none of us
is tired enough to sleep, we pull out the old
carousel slide projector and look at pictures.
Most of them seem to be Dad's work pictures of trees
with diseased leaves, but then we find some good ones.

We are all so young and beautiful
with our pouts and our smiles. We are splashing
in the waves and running through the Japanese
gardens in San Francisco. Our mom turns
on a bridge and smiles at us over her shoulder.
We decide to sleep in the living room
and have a slumber party.
Tomorrow we pack for an overnight
in Cape May before we take Meg
to her residential program outside of Philly.
There she'll continue her recovery
focusing on the eating disorders this time.
Dad is totally committed to her treatment.
I listen to him all the time now
with my eyes.

Meg

Homecoming is strange. How long have I been away? At the first sign of the crystal goblets Maura has on the table, I go call my sponsor, Annie. When I come back, I can tell Maura's worried and suspicious about my absence.

"Relax," I tell her. "I'm going to have to call my sponsor and check in, and I have to go to a meeting at 7:30. It's right at our church in Glyndon; you can come, if you want. It's an open meeting."

"It's just when you go upstairs..." she says.

"I know," I say, "but you're going to have to trust me a little."

"I just don't want anything to go wrong while you're home. They made Dad sign all these disclaimers."

I don't mean to, but I get bristly, "Look, Maura. Recovery is my responsibility. I am the one responsible."

"You do seem different."

"Living sober is different, that's for sure—a little less fun, a little embarrassing. You wouldn't believe all the rules," I tell her.

"I want to follow the rules, too, if it will help," she says.

"I appreciate that, but you don't have to. I wouldn't mind if you went with me to the meeting, though. You'd like Annie, my sponsor, if you could meet her. She reminds me of you a little, except she's not so annoying," I joke.

"Wait a minute," she says. "*I'm* not the annoying sister."

"We can all be pretty damned annoying," I say.

"Can't argue with you there," she agrees.

It seems right that we head to the beach the next day, even though we can't go to Ocean City anymore. The accident haunts us, but so does the thought that Mom loved the beach, and we don't have to cross the Bay Bridge to get to Cape May.

Cape May is a magical place, a gingerbread village with real gardens and trees a hundred years old right on the Atlantic Ocean. Real people seem to live here, too. No taffy shacks or go-cart amusements. Just big white houses with porches that seem inviting, even in December.

We arrive early in the day and take a giant step out of reality. We find coffee in a general store and take it to the beach. It's a mild day, despite the season, and the sun is starting to peek through.

Mia throws her shoes off and runs. I pick them up and start filling one of them up with tiny shells and small crystals. We walk for an hour, not really talking, focused on the water, letting the waves splash our clothes.

The ocean always reminds me of my mother: beautiful, stormy, a little wild and salty. She's here, I think, but she's in me, too. She was hard on me and we clashed, but she loved me.

We're here together swirling in the chilly air. There's the sound of crashing waves instead of conversation, and that works for us.

The days ahead are going to be hard, but I feel a certainty that I'm not alone in this. There is something greater at work, something I can't explain. I think Mom has something to do with it. I feel that Mom forgives me— that she wants me to get on with my life. She's more a presence in my life than ever before. I can turn to her now. I can hear her voice and her laughter. I feel certain that she lives, and I'll see her again. She's picking out the pattern for my next dress; she's crocheting a shawl to warm my shoulders.

So, I'm ready to keep counting. My clean and sober days, my days of feeding myself. I know what giving up looks like—Ruth with a swollen belly, a bleeding brain. If I need to scare myself into a good choice, I think of that.

My most important relationship is with myself. I believe that now, but I also want to do this for my Dad, walking beside me on the beach, helping me find diamonds in the sand. I can't let him face another loss, not after all he's been through and done for me. He gives me so much and never complains. I can't imagine why he thinks I'm worth it, but he does.

Dad is disappointed with the fried clams we have for lunch. Nobody has those good clams anymore. Three of us drink club soda, but Mia has a Coke. Mia talks about how she wants to move in with her boyfriend, Danny. He has a rented apartment but drives every day on a John Deere tractor from his apartment to the family farm. Mia likes riding along beside him.

Maura seems a little uptight. She should learn to take a joke, and we are a joke. The four of us, we could be a sitcom.

We head west to Philadelphia following a bright moon. I hope I'll get to the point where I can help someone else, like Rob with the shaggy hair. He left me a voicemail yesterday—"Just calling to see how you're doing. I know someone at Oak Park, if you need a friend."

I've lost count of how many times I've listened to his message. To me, his voice says, *you aren't alone, and you aren't a loser, and you aren't hopeless, and you are worth my time.*

His voice is canceling out the old voice in my head. The one that told me I was worthless, not thin enough, not pretty or smart enough, not worth the trouble.

I wonder if he means anything by calling or if he's just being a good counselor and doing his job? I plan to make sure it's been a full year of sobriety, but I do think eventually, I'll give him a call.

Maura

I have a moment of panic
as we walk on the beach.
What would I do
without my sister, Meg?
She's the one I can talk to.
Dad and Mia are sweet, of course,
but they are just hard work.
Look at Mia right now:
she's pulling up her gauzy skirt
and showing her underwear.
It's winter and she's going to get
herself soaked and she doesn't
even have a change of clothes.
And with Dad, you never know
what he's going to do.
Last week he gave Mom's sewing machine
to some strange woman
he met at the American Legion.
He doesn't even know what day it is
half the time.

Meg looks so fragile,
but she's the strong one.
She's the organized and ambitious one.
The one who's going places.
And she's the reason
I've been able to go
to college for four years
and graduate school now.
She's the reason I have

the freedom I have.
She's taken care of the house
and everyone in it
since Mom's been gone.
I want to thank her
and tell her that I love her
but she's lost in her own thoughts
right now, and I don't want to interrupt.

My mother is here in the waves.
I'm sorry,
I say to the waves.
I'll be a better sister,
I say to the wind.
We still need you,
I say to the salty air.

Meg
1985
Somewhere in Philadelphia

Out on the street today, some homeless guy starts shouting at me, "Do you know that you've been saved?" I smell his sour breath. My heart starts beating faster, and I run—stumble, really—back to the house. The whole episode freaked me out, but all day, I keep hearing that old guy's question in my head.

I could have told him, *I do know I've been saved.* I was saved exactly one hundred thirty-two days ago. One hundred thirty-two days and counting.

One hundred thirty-two days ago, I was supposed to get married. I was supposed to wear my mother's lacy wedding gown and make my sisters wear royal blue bridesmaid dresses. Dad was supposed to walk me down the aisle. Getting married was supposed to make everything right again. But I didn't get married, I got *saved* instead. My hero snatched me right from the jaws of the angry yellow dragon.

All of this might sound crazy. A sordid fairy tale. A lurid soap opera. Too bizarre to be true. But with my heart beating too fast and my whole body still feeling the breath of the angry dragon, this is my story.

Acknowledgements

Although I cannot name everyone who supported me over the years it has taken to write this book, I appreciate every gesture of encouragement and kind word I have received.

The story told here is deeply personal, and the characters are based in part on the real members of my birth family. We were flawed souls who loved each other and could throw a good party. I am grateful for the lessons I keep learning from them, and I am glad I still have my sister Molly.

Immense gratitude goes out to counselors and mental health professionals who help people suffering from inherited disorders. I am grateful for every stigma lifted and by every broken spirit healed.

I might have lost my way entirely if not for the poetry and teaching of Elizabeth Spires and a poet she introduced me to, Kathy Mangan. Joan Fowler coached me through teacher training, found me a husband and a job, and still tells me all the important books to read. The influence of these three women in my life cannot be overstated.

Special thanks to Mary Beth Seal, Lisa Jaworski, Ellie Miklich, and Tracy Sanna for reading drafts of the book and for all the positive energy they send my way.

The following writers provided me with invaluable critical feedback: Andrea Shalal, MacKerrow Talcott, Holli Chadwick, Corinne Zibell, Hannah Zinn, Julie Bohaska, Kathleen Shemer, Mary Beth Stuller, Linda Johnson, Evelyn Fazio, and Kendra Kopelke.

Linda Johnson's immense range of talents improved

the book. She offered careful readings of the text, technical expertise, and she designed and painted the lovely watercolor for the cover. I thank her and her husband Dave for sharing the cabin at Garden Gate Farm for a long writing retreat where some of this book was written.

Thanks to Mary Beth Stuller who encouraged me to submit the manuscript to Atmosphere Press. Everyone at Atmosphere Press has earned my respect and admiration. I especially want to acknowledge the work of Nick Court-right and Alex Kale. They are extraordinary editors, and the way they conduct business is a bright spot in the world of publishing.

Kendra Kopelke could write her own better version of this story—she lived it all with me. I thank her for answering each question and mentoring me with honesty. I thank her for introducing me to new sister poets, for making everything more fun, and for a million other things.

I thank my dear sons, Burke and Samuel, for being my reason to keep trying every day. They light up this dark world.

Tim Stanton is at the top of the list of people for whom I am most thankful. Because he takes such good care of me, I had all the time and space I needed to write and rewrite this story.

About Atmosphere Press

Atmosphere Press is an independent, full-service publisher for excellent books in all genres and for all audiences. Learn more about what we do at atmospherepress.com.

We encourage you to check out some of Atmosphere's latest releases, which are available at Amazon.com and via order from your local bookstore:

Relatively Painless, short stories by Dylan Brody
Nate's New Age, a novel by Michael Hanson
The Size of the Moon, a novel by E.J. Michaels
The Red Castle, a novel by Noah Verhoeff
American Genes, a novel by Kirby Nielsen
Newer Testaments, a novel by Philip Brunetti
All Things in Time, a novella by Sue Buyer
Hobson's Mischief, a novel by Caitlin Decatur
The Black-Marketer's Daughter, a novel by Suman Mallick
The Farthing Quest, a novel by Casey Bruce
This Side of Babylon, a novel by James Stoia
Within the Gray, a novel by Jenna Ashlyn
Where No Man Pursueth, a novel by Micheal E. Jimerson
Here's Waldo, a novel by Nick Olson
Tales of Little Egypt, a historical novel by James Gilbert
For a Better Life, a novel by Julia Reid Galosy
The Hidden Life, a novel by Robert Castle
Big Beasts, a novel by Patrick Scott
Alvarado, a novel by John W. Horton III

About the Author

Katy Stanton is a Maryland writer who grew up in rural Baltimore County and still finds the landscape of her childhood inspirational to her work. A graduate of Washington College and Johns Hopkins University's Writing Seminars, she taught English in Baltimore County Public Schools for 30 years and currently teaches writing at McDaniel College. Stanton is the mother of two adult sons, and she lives in Westminster, Maryland with her husband Tim and her dog Shadow. *Say Hello* is her first novel.